# The Unexpected Bride

Hope's Crossing, Book 4

# CYNTHIA WOOLF

ISBN: 1938887832
ISBN- 978-1-938887-83-3

# DEDICATION

For Jim. Thank you for being my greatest cheerleader, my husband, my lover and my best friend.

I love you, sweetheart!

# ACKNOWLEDGMENTS

For my Just Write partners Michele Callahan, Karen Docter, and Cate  Rowan

For my wonderful cover artist, Romcon Custom Covers

For my wonderful editor, Linda Carroll-Bradd, you make my stories so much better.

# CHAPTER 1

April 2, 1873

Dr. Jeremiah "Doc" Kilarney needed help. As the only doctor in Hope's Crossing and nearby Nevada City, both in the Montana Territory, he was kept more than busy, trying to care for the 3000 residents who live within the two towns. With those thoughts in mind, he writes an advertisement to send to the newspapers in New York, San Francisco and Denver.

*Nurse/wife wanted to aid doctor in Hope's Crossing, a mining town in the Montana Territory. Woman should have training as a nurse or willing to learn. Marriage will take place on arrival. Write to Dr. Kilarney, General Delivery, Hope's Crossing, Montana Territory.*

*That ought to do it. This way I don't*

*have to court them and they won't be expecting me to love them, because that's not happening. I'll never love again. Susan broke me of that tender emotion when she abandoned me. I couldn't help my time away in the war and she said she understood. But that was a lie. She was just waiting for Howard Blake to come around and marry her. Well, he wouldn't be fooled again.*

He copied the missive three times and put each one in an envelope. He addressed one to the New York Times, one to the Rocky Mountain News in Denver and one to the San Francisco Chronicle for their personal classifieds. Then he walked it over to the hotel to give the three envelopes to Miss Effie, who served as postmistress.

Effie stood behind the hotel registration desk. She was less than five feet tall with shiny silver hair pulled up into a bun high on her head and even standing only her head was visible above the tall counter.

"New York Times? Rocky Mountain News? San Francisco Chronicle? What's going on, Doc? You gonna get yourself a subscription to them papers?"

"No, if you must know, I'm advertising for a nurse and wife. I realize that any woman that comes here would constantly be bombarded with offers of matrimony, so I am proposing to marry her as soon as she arrives. I don't need my nurse being distracted. I need her to help me."

"Kind of like a mail-order bride, except you aren't goin' through the agency. Maybe you should."

"You think so?"

"Jesse, Sam and Alex did just fine with that Matchmaker & Company agency. Maybe before you send these you ought to talk to them, huh? That agency can find you a nurse a lot more surely than just posting in these papers for one."

"You may have something there, Effie. I wouldn't have to sort through lots of letters. I could just give the owner of the agency my requirements. He can then see that they are met by the woman."

"That's right. Why don't you go talk to Jo or Clare and get the address of that agency?"

"I will. Thanks, Effie. I needed to go see Jo, anyway."

He tucked the envelopes into his coat pocket and left the hotel headed for the sheriff's house. When he arrived he knocked on the door.

A pretty, heavily pregnant blonde woman answered the door.

"Hello there, Doc. Come on in. Sam's in the kitchen. Why don't you give me your coat, and then go on in and get yourself a cup of coffee?"

"Sounds good, Jo. I'd like to talk to you both."

He took off his coat and handed it to Jo Longworth then walked into the kitchen.

Sam Longworth, the town sheriff, sat at the table eating his breakfast.

"Hello, Doc. Help yourself to coffee. Are you hungry? Jo can whip up some eggs."

"That's right," said Jo from behind him. "You just sit there and let me get some food prepared. You look like you need some good cooking."

He poured a cup of coffee and sat at the table across from Sam. "Thank you. I'd love some cooking that isn't my own. My cooking, what I do of it, leaves something to be desired."

"That says a lot as to why you're so thin," said Jo, pointing a spatula at him.

"Now what else can we do for you,

Doc?" Sam set his fork on his plate and lifted his coffee cup to his lips.

"I wanted to ask you about your mail-order bride company. I need a nurse but I can't have a single woman in this town if I want to get any work done, so I've decided to marry her."

Jo brought the coffee pot to the table and topped off both his and Sam's cups. "And you want to know if Matchmaker & Co. can find you a nurse to marry, right?"

"That's it exactly."

"I don't see why they wouldn't be able to. The agency has offices in New York City and Golden, in the Colorado Territory, and they have ladies who apply to them from all over. I was in Illinois when I wrote to them," said Jo. "After breakfast I'll sit down with you and we'll write a letter to Mrs. Black."

"I want to check you over, too, while I'm here. See how that baby is doing."

"He's fine, Doc. Moves around a lot, especially when I'm trying to sleep."

Doc chuckled. "Sounds about right. At this time in your pregnancy, the little one should be moving around a lot. I'd be worried if it wasn't."

"*He,* Doc. It's a boy, I know it is." Jo placed her hand on her belly.

"Very well, *he.* You should still be about a month out, if our calculations were correct."

She brushed the hair from her forehead with the back of her hand. "I'm ready for him to be born now."

*Poor Jo. This last month is the hardest according to my other patients.* "I know. All you expectant mothers get to feeling that way about this time, but the baby will come when he's ready and not before."

Jo spooned the scrambled eggs from the skillet to a plate and set it in front of him.

Doc rubbed his hands together and reached for the salt and pepper. Then he took a bite of the fluffy eggs and smiled.

"These are great, Jo."

"Here's toast and bacon, too." She set another plate with those offerings in front of him.

No one talked while they all ate their breakfast.

Finally, when Jo was done, she got up and took her dishes to the sink. Then she left the kitchen, returning shortly with a sheet of paper, pen and ink.

"Okay, Doc, what do you want to say to Mrs. Black?"

He pulled out the envelopes from his pocket, opened one and pulled out the single sheet of paper.

"This is what I was sending to the newspapers. He read out loud. '*Nurse/wife wanted to aid doctor in Hope's Crossing, a mining town in the Montana Territory. Woman should be trained as a nurse or willing to learn. Marriage will take place on arrival. Write to Dr. Kilarney, General Delivery, Hope's Crossing, Montana Territory.*'

"What I really need is a woman who will be willing to work beside me in a medical capacity as my nurse and also be my wife. Cooking abilities would be great. Do you think your Mrs. Black could find me someone like that?"

"I think so. Let me write up something."

Jo spent the next few minutes writing on the paper. Finally, she looked up from her task.

"Okay, tell me what you think."

*April 2, 1873*

*Dear Mrs. Black,*

*Jo Longworth here. I'm writing on*

*behalf of my friend, Doctor Jeremiah Kilarney. Doc is in need of a wife, but she must be a nurse or someone willing to learn and work alongside the doctor. Cooking skills would be much appreciated, but are not required.*

*The woman would be located in Hope's Crossing where the doctor lives. As I may have mentioned in my letters to you, Hope's Crossing is not a large town though it provides us with everything we need and more. Anything she wants can be purchased at the mercantile or ordered through them.*

*Dr. Kilarney is thirty-eight years old, average height and slim. He has graying hair and kind gray eyes. He also has all his teeth and is able to provide for a wife, though he is not a rich man.*

*Please write back to Dr. Jeremiah Kilarney, General Delivery, Hope's Crossing, Montana Territory.*

*Sincerely,*

*Jo Longworth and Dr. Jeremiah Kilarney*

"Well? What do you think?" she asked.

"That sounds good to me. Do you really think she can help me?"

"Let's put it this way, if she can't I don't

know who can."

*****

May 1, 1873

Alice Carter wore her best lavender silk dress which she knew made her violet eyes appear even more purple than normal. The cool May weather forced her to cover her lovely dress with a black wool overcoat. The calendar may say the season was spring but the weather was still more like winter with the cold and recent snow New Yorkers had to endure.

It was too soon for her to be wearing lavender, she was in mourning and should still be wearing black for another six months, then six months of gray and then six months of lavender, but she couldn't stick with tradition. She'd worn black to the other interviews she'd had and hadn't gotten the job. Today, she had to find a husband and that didn't involve wearing mourning.

She stood in front of the bright blue door at 221 Baker Street, taking deep breaths to calm her nerves. Apparently she wasn't too successful, as her hand still shook when she turned the door knob.

A bell above the door rang as she

entered.

"Hello. Come on in," said a pretty brunette woman, with spectacles, from behind a large oak desk.

Her voice was husky, pleasant to the ear and put Alice at ease. "Thank you."

She glanced around at the sparse but serviceable furnishings. A pot-bellied stove in one corner, two tables topped with boxes of files behind the desk and a single ladder back wooden chair in front of the desk. She made her way into the room and sat in the chair.

"I'm Sally Wyatt." She folded her hands on the top of the desk. "I manage this office of Matchmaker & Co. What can we do for you, Miss…"

"Carter. Mrs. Alice Carter. I'm here because I want to become a mail-order bride."

"I assumed," she said with a smile and reached for a form. "I don't get too many female visitors who want something else. So tell me why you want to make use of our matching services?"

With a lump in her throat, Alice pressed on. "Well, I'm recently widowed and a doctor. I graduated from the Women's

Medical College of Pennsylvania. I'm unable to find a position using my skills here in the city and thought that if I went west where doctors are in demand, that I might be able to use my knowledge to help people."

"I'm so sorry for your loss. What is your living situation like here?"

Alice found it hard to talk about the time with Adam. It seemed like he'd been gone so long, because she missed him so much. But this needed to happen.

"When my husband died we were renting a house and looking for one to buy. I've gone through our savings in the last six months, just paying for rent and food and his funeral. I've tried to find a position but no one wants a widow who is still in mourning."

Sally looked at Alice for a moment, with her finger on her chin.

"Would you be willing to accept the position of a nurse to your doctor husband? At least until you can convince him of your medical training?"

"Yes. Anything to get my patients familiar with me so they will have an easier time accepting me as a doctor."

Sally made notes on a piece of paper and

examined papers from a folder on the desk.

"Wonderful. I have a doctor in Hope's Crossing. It's a very small mining town in Montana Territory. He is thirty-eight years old. How old are you?"

"I'm twenty-nine."

"Do you have experience as a practicing doctor?"

Alice shook her head. "Not really. Right after I graduated I married Adam Carter. We'd known each other a long time. He was also a doctor. When I finished my two-year residency, I discovered I was expecting Melly...Melissa...my daughter. After Melissa was born, I didn't want to go to work and Adam was making a nice living."

She stopped, closed her eyes for a moment. This was so hard. She didn't know how she would keep from breaking down. Then she thought of Melly and knew she must keep herself together. There was no choice.

"Are you sure this is what you want to do?"

"Miss Wyatt, my husband passed away six months ago. I haven't been able to find a position here and I need to provide for Melly, who is three now. Our savings are running out, I must do this."

"Hmm. I understand. There is a little more of an age difference than I usually allow for our matches, and I hadn't planned for a child, but he didn't exclude his bride from having one. With you both being doctors, you should have plenty in common to talk about. I think you will get along. Can you cook?"

"I'm a good cook but I don't want to just be the cook and housekeeper."

"No, I don't imagine you do. Let me give you his letter."

Sally rummaged through the stack of file folders on her desk. When she found the one she was looking for she pulled out a single sheet of creased paper and handed it to Alice.

"Jo Longworth is a former client and very happy in the match we made for her."

Alice read the letter, before looking up and giving back the sheet of paper to Sally, who tucked it into the folder.

"Well? What do you think?"

"I think he'll do. Can you arrange it?"

She nodded. "I'll write to him and to the owner of the company, Mrs. Maggie Black. She lives in Golden in the Colorado

Territory and runs another office out of that town."

"When do I leave for Montana Territory?"

"I want you to write a response to Dr. Kilarney. I'll make arrangements for train and stagecoach tickets as soon as possible and I'll send you a message when they are ready for pick up. You should be packed and ready to go."

"Very well. I don't have much. A few clothes and some small things that have memories attached, plus Melly's clothes and doll. A couple of valises is all we'll need."

"Fine. That makes it easier. Plan on leaving on the ten o'clock train to Chicago in ten days. You'll change trains in Chicago to go on to Cheyenne in the Wyoming Territory. The stagecoach to Hope's Crossing takes seven or eight days. It's definitely not an easy trip. Are you sure you're up for it? With a small child along, the travel will be that much more difficult."

"We'll be fine. Melly is a good traveler. She makes friends with everyone."

"All right then, be back here in two hours to pick up your tickets."

"I will. Thank you very much for your

help."

"It's not a problem. That's what I'm here for. Now hurry home and do whatever you need to do."

"I'm leaving. See you then."

Feelings of sadness and excitement warred in her brain. Sadness that she was leaving the only place she'd ever lived. She had many memories of her and Adam when they were first married, in that tiny apartment above an Italian restaurant.

After Melly was born they moved to a small house close to the hospital. They'd just gotten together money to be able to reach upward again and buy their own house when Adam was killed.

*No. I won't think about that or about Adam. I have to do this. I must provide for Melly...and for myself.*

She stepped into the street to cross when a carriage came galloping toward her. The driver wasn't slowing. As a matter of fact she saw the whip in his hand and heard him crack it over the horse's heads.

Alice froze she couldn't move. Just watched it coming closer. Just as it was upon her, a strong arm pulled her back into a hard chest.

"Miss. Are you all right? You could have been killed." A deep masculine voice accompanied the arm.

She turned in his arms and looked up into dark blue eyes in a very handsome face with strong jaw.

"Daniel? Is that you?"

"Alice. What are you doing down here? I heard about Adam. I'm very sorry for your loss."

"I had business to conduct. How are Priscilla and the children?"

"They're fine. Come let's get some hot tea in you and we can talk."

She couldn't believe it. Daniel Jameson. How long had it been since she'd seen her old beau? Years.

They stopped at a little eatery and went inside.

After they were seated, Daniel started the conversation.

"You look good, Alice. I see you're out of mourning."

"Only out of necessity. No one wants to hire a widow still in mourning."

"No, I don't suppose they do. Now why don't you tell me why someone would want to run you down?"

"There is only one person who might want to, the same man who killed Adam. Dick Lane."

"You should report it to the police."

"I will, though they won't be able to do anything about it. Lane is long gone. The carriage he used was probably stolen. What are you doing in New York? Are Priscilla and the boys with you?"

"I'm here for a conference. I'm actually leaving today, in about two hours."

"Well, I'm glad you were here to save me. I would have been killed or at the very least maimed."

"I'm glad I was here, too."

After they'd drank their tea, Alice stood.

Daniel followed suit.

"I have to go collect Melly and then have packing to do."

"Are you sure you're making the right decision to be a mail-order bride?"

"It's the right decision for me, at this time."

"Well, take care of yourself and be sure and report that incident to the police. I have to catch a cab to the station or I'll miss my train. Keep in touch."

"I'll try. Goodbye. Tell Pris hello for

me."

He laughed.

"I won't even mention I saw you or I'll get the third degree and she won't believe me anyway. Not enough water under the bridge for Pris. She still remembers that I courted you first."

"Until Adam swept me off my feet."

He nodded. "Yes, until Adam."

"Take care, Daniel." She stood on tiptoe and kissed his cheek.

"You, too, Alice."

\*\*\*\*\*

She put Dick Lane and Daniel Jameson out of her mind. In her real life she had a daughter she loved and needed to take care of. Tomorrow she would go to the police, but for now she picked up Melly from the neighbor, a little old woman who loved having her, and went home. There she looked around carefully and pulled only the things she couldn't live without off the walls and out of drawers. She'd contact the landlord about the rest. He could sell it and keep the money for his trouble. She didn't think it would bring much.

In her closet she pulled out the most serviceable of her dresses and the most colorful. She took one black bombazine dress, one purple made from heavy silk, two cotton skirts one brown and one lavender, along with their matching shirtwaists. She also managed to get two pairs of bloomers, two petty coats and two corsets. That was it, the bag was full.

In the second bag she was able to get Melly's clothes, doll, a picture of her father. Alice added two more skirts and shirtwaists for herself, and one totally unneeded royal purple evening gown. She knew she shouldn't take it, but it was her favorite dress out of all of them and if nothing else, she'd wear it to cook dinner if she had to. But maybe there would be a dance or some other occasion for her to wear it.

Now that she was packed and ready to go, she went to talk to Mr. Martin, the landlord, about selling off the furnishings. She'd take her and Adam's clothes to the church herself. She needed to let the pastor know she was leaving, anyway.

# CHAPTER 2

May 12, 1873

As he stood on the boardwalk in front of the hotel, Doc was more nervous than if he'd been performing surgery for the first time. He took off his hat, wiped his handkerchief over his forehead and cursed the lack of clouds in the clear, blue sky before returning his hat to his head.

His bride should be arriving on the morning stage. He'd received a wire from Matchmaker & Co., stating Alice Carter would be in Hope's Crossing on the eleventh or twelfth of May. Since she hadn't arrived on yesterday's stage, she should be on today's.

He had Judge Nate Hardin standing by to perform the ceremony as soon as Alice arrived. Doc was marrying her as quickly as possible so he could get back to his duties.

The stage pulled up in front of the hotel and the only woman who got out was a very short blonde. She was about five feet and two inches, if that, and accompanied by a small child, who looked just like her. A child? He hadn't expected a child. Had she said there was a daughter? Did he forget a detail like that? Hopefully the little girl would like him and there would be no problems. He walked over to them.

At the same moment, the driver handed two valises to the shotgun rider who set them on the boardwalk beside the woman.

"There you are, Mrs. Carter," said the man. "Goodbye, Melly."

"Bye, Mister Driver," called the little girl, waving.

The driver waved back.

The man tipped his hat to Mrs. Carter and then climbed back aboard the stagecoach headed for the next stop.

Doc stepped up to the woman and removed his hat, holding it tightly in his hands. "Mrs. Carter? Alice Carter?"

"I'm Alice Carter and this is my daughter, Melissa. We…I…call her Melly."

The woman smiled down at her daughter

and patted the hand she held.

"Are you Jeremiah Kilarney?"

"I am. I've arranged for us to be married right away."

Her hand flew to her throat and she backed up a step. "Not so fast, Doctor Kilarney. I want us to know a bit about each other, and we're hungry. Is there some place we can go to get a meal and talk for a bit?"

Doc was surprised at her firm disposition. She appeared to be a strong-willed woman. That would work out well if she was to help him. If trouble happened during one of his visits, she could take care of the distraught family.

He looked down at the girl. She was a pretty little thing, standing there holding her doll with one hand and her mother's hand with the other. He smiled.

She smiled back, showing two adorable dimples in her cheeks. She edged out away from her mother toward Doc...and kicked him in the shin.

"Melly!" Mrs. Carter grabbed her daughter and put the child behind her. "I'm so sorry. I don't know what got into her. Normally she's a very nice child." Alice turned and knelt in front of her daughter.

"That was very bad of you. You will get no dessert at dinner."

The child's chin went from mutinous to quivering. Tears ran down her face.

"Why did you kick this nice man?"

The girl shrugged and shook her head.

"We will talk about this later. In the mean time, you apologize at once or you will go without dinner completely."

Shin throbbing and impressed by her method of discipline, he moved forward a step. "Please Mrs. Carter. She didn't hurt me. I'm sure she feels threatened by me. She's been through difficult trip as have you. I've taken the stage to Cheyenne on several occasions and it's not a journey I would choose to make again."

"It is true the travel was difficult, but that's no excuse for her to kick you."

"Why don't we see how she and I get on after a good supper and a full night's sleep? I'm sure all will be better tomorrow."

"Well, if you're sure, but she still must apologize." Frowning, she looked down at her daughter and jutted her chin toward Doc.

"Sorry," said the little girl as she looked at the ground and swung side to side.

"You are forgiven. Now, the restaurant

here at the hotel is good. I'll leave your bags at the desk. They'll watch them."

"That sounds fine," said Mrs. Carter.

Doc picked up her bags and carried them inside.

Mrs. Carter and Melly followed.

"Clarence," said Doc to the redheaded young man behind the desk. "We're headed to the restaurant. Will you watch these bags?"

"Sure thing, Doc."

Clarence picked up the bags and stashed them under the desk.

"They'll be right here, in case I'm away when you return."

"Thank you. We'll be back as soon as we get some sustenance into Mrs. Carter and her daughter, here." He pointed at the woman he already thought of as Alice. He liked the name. Simple, yet pretty.

Alice, Melly and Doc went into the restaurant and Effie seated them at a table.

"What can I get for you three?"

"Just water for me, milk for Melly," said Alice.

"Water for me, too, Effie," said Doc.

"Sure thing. Be right back," said the little woman.

After Effie left, Doc looked across the table at Alice. "All right what would you like to know, Mrs. Carter? Or may I call you Alice?"

"Alice is fine. Why are you still single at your age? Surely you've run across women of the marriageable variety."

He lifted his eyebrows. "I've never had the time to court a woman before marrying her. That's why I wanted a mail-order bride."

"I thought you wanted a nurse and were to marry her only because you had to."

"That's true. You're a nurse are you not?"

"No."

"Well, I did also ask for someone willing to learn. Are you willing?"

"No."

He rubbed his hands over his face. *I must not be angry.* "Then what was the point of you coming here? Surely not to marry me. There were probably a lot of more eligible men than me."

Alice folded her hands on the table and aimed her violet gaze at Doc.

"I'm sorry for misleading you with the question about the nurse. Actually, I'm a doctor. I graduated from the Women's Medical College of Pennsylvania and I want to practice medicine. As you know from the letter Miss Wyatt sent you, I lost my husband six months ago and have been unable to find a position in New York. I came here hoping my skills would help you and that we could work together."

Doc's eyes had widened when she first said she was a doctor then he narrowed them. A doctor? Not likely.

"That's very impressive Alice, but I didn't want another doctor, I wanted a nurse to help me with my patients, not to take them over."

He should get up and leave but he didn't. Instead he listened to her.

She locked her gaze with his. "I'm willing to act as your nurse until you feel you can trust me to be otherwise."

Doc put his elbow on the table and then rested his chin in his hand while he stared at her.

"I need a nurse. Badly. Otherwise, I wouldn't be thinking of taking you up on your offer."

"And," she prompted when she apparently thought he'd waited too long to finish his thought.

"And I'm willing to give it a try. We'll marry as we intended and you'll start helping with my patients."

Effie stepped up to the table with the drinks.

"Who are these pretty ladies with you, Doc?"

He waved his hand toward Alice. "This is Mrs. Alice Carter and her daughter, Melly. Mrs. Carter came all the way from New York City to be my bride."

"Congratulations, and I'm pleased to meet you Alice. I'm Effie Smith, I own the hotel and this restaurant. I also run the post office and the newspaper."

"Pleased to meet you Miss Smith. How do you keep up with so many duties? I'm exhausted just thinking about it."

"It's Effie. I'm long past being Miss Smith and doing all those things is what keeps me young. Now what can I get you all to eat?"

Alice looked up at the chalkboard with the menu written on it. "I'd like the steak and eggs, with the eggs over easy, fried potatoes and toast. For my daughter, a bowl of oatmeal, please."

"That sounds wonderful," said Doc. "I'll have the same as Mrs. Carter."

"How do you want your steaks?"

"Medium," replied Doc and Alice at the same time.

They looked at each other and laughed.

"Well, all right then. Medium, it is."

Effie turned and headed back toward the kitchen.

Alice looked at Doc. "Back to our conversation. What if you decide the partnership is not working, we'll still be married."

"Then we can either stay married or get an annulment."

She lifted an eyebrow. "What if the situation is such that we can no longer get an annulment?"

He took a deep breath. "Then we could get a divorce."

"I don't believe in divorce."

"Well, then we'd stay married and you'd continue as my nurse and we'll see about the other."

Alice narrowed her eyes and then looked down at her daughter.

"All right, you've got yourself a deal, Jeremiah."

"Call me Doc. Everyone does."

"Only in public when you're working. But at home or when we are alone, you'll be Jeremiah."

"Deal, Alice Carter. Shake on it." He extended his hand.

She shook his hand and he was surprised at her firm grip.

A couple of minutes later, their food came.

"Shall we eat and then go see the judge?" asked Jeremiah.

She nodded. "That will be perfect."

Alice put cream and sugar on her daughter's oatmeal.

Doc cut into his steak, found it cooked perfectly. It was tender, juicy and delicious.

"How is your steak?"

"Wonderful. That's the first time I've ever gotten my steak done as I like it on the first try. It's usually too rare."

"You've got quite the appetite for such a small lady."

She smiled.

"Don't let my size fool you, I'm strong and I work hard. I'll be able to help you, Jeremiah. Just give me the chance."

"Oh, you'll get your chance. By the time

we get back to the office, the waiting room will be full. So eat up." He pointed at her plate. "I want you to triage the patients and send them back to see me."

"I don't see that as being a problem."

"You will when you see how many people are present."

"Do you have set hours for in-office patients?"

"No."

"Why not? Doctors in the city do and they have more patients than you simply because they are in a big city. I understand for house calls such as births that you couldn't have office hours." She cocked her head to one side. "But for regular things like colds and the flu, you most definitely could. Having them would ease some of the chaos in your life."

He sat back in his chair. "You don't have any idea whether I have chaos in my life or not. You just got here."

"You're right. But from everything you've been telling me…how many people will be waiting and how I'll be so busy…I can only conclude that you have some chaos in your practice. I'm simply following your descriptions to the logical conclusion."

He sighed and pinched the skin between his eyebrows. "Well, I'm willing to do this. Are you?"

"I didn't come all this way to just go back. Even as your nurse I'll be able to help people and that is what I want to do."

"Then if you two are finished with your meals I suggest we go see Judge Harden."

"I agree."

She put her napkin on the table next to her plate, took Melly's napkin, dipped it in her water glass and cleaned the little girl's face. Then they both stood.

Doc held out his arm to escort her out of the hotel and down two blocks to the only brick building in town.

She shook her head.

"Thank you, but I like to be able to help Melly if she trips." She took the child's hand and the three walked to the courthouse.

They walked in and Jeremiah went directly to the judge's office.

"Hello, William."

Doc glanced at the partially open door to the judge's chambers. "Is the judge ready for us?"

"He is but I need some information for the marriage license before you go inside."

"All right what do you need?"

"Your full names including your middle name, please."

"Jeremiah Raymond Kilarney."

"Alice Elizabeth Carter.

"Thank you. You can go on in. I'll be there in a moment. I have to go get Sarah from the office next door."

Alice picked up Melly, and then she and Jeremiah walked through the partially open door.

"Doc. Glad to see you're taking the plunge." He looked over at Alice. "And with such a pretty lady, too."

She blushed, her cheeks a nice rosy pink.

"Thank you, sir."

Melly pointed at the judge. "Santa."

He laughed. "I get that a lot from the little ones. Don't call me sir or judge or anything except Nate."

"Very well, you can call me Alice and this is Melly."

Nate stood and walked around the desk to stand in front of them. "Alice it will be. Hello Melly."

"Hello," said Melly. She didn't hide from Nate and Doc was sure it was because she thought he was Santa Clause.

"Tell me Alice, does Doc make you call him Doc or Jeremiah? He's made all of us use Doc."

"I told him I'd use Doc in public and Jeremiah in private."

"Looks like you got a keeper here, Doc. Pretty and smart."

"You've no idea," said Jeremiah.

"Well, let's get you two married. You stand right there facing me. When Clarence and Sarah...ah, there they are." He spoke to the two young people who had just entered the office. "You two know what to do."

Sarah walked over next to Alice and Clarence stood next to Doc.

"That's right," said Nate. "Let's start. Dearly beloved, we are gathered here in front of these witnesses..."

The judge intoned with the ceremony until he suddenly stopped.

Doc cleared his throat and nodded to Alice.

"I do," she said quickly.

"Then by the power vested in me, by the Territory of Montana, I now pronounce you man and wife. You may kiss the bride."

Jeremiah bent down and gave her a

quick peck on the lips.

It was not the kiss she may have hoped for on her wedding day but he supposed it was all right. After all, he could have kissed her on the cheek, instead.

He turned to Nate, "What do I owe you?

"A free visit next time my daughter, Sadie, needs you." The judge rocked back on his heels with his thumbs hooked in his pockets. "She's expecting you know."

"I'm the one who told her she was going to have another baby."

Shaking his head, Nate laughed. "Yes, I guess you were."

Doc waved toward the door. "We need to get to the office. There will be a dozen people waiting."

Alice nodded to the judge. "It was very nice to meet you, Nate. I hope we'll see you around town and not in the office."

"Right you are, young lady."

Doc went to the door and held it open for Alice. Melly walked beside her mother.

"Goodbye Nate. See you at the poker game," said Jeremiah.

"That you will and I expect a chance to get my money back."

*****

34

Jeremiah laughed.

It was a deep, rich sound much like his speaking voice was. Alice liked the way he sounded. There was authority in his voice and his patients would appreciate that. They would listen to him, just from the way he told them to take their medicine or moderate their activity.

"Bye, Santa." Melly waved her hand.

"Goodbye, Melly. Be a good girl for your mama."

Melly nodded vigorously. "I will."

Alice took Melly's hand and kept walking until they were in the hallway.

Jeremiah came abreast of her and picked up her valises with one hand. His other arm swept around to include everything.

"Welcome to Hope's Crossing Alice Kilarney."

She looked up the street, saw the six or so businesses that weren't whorehouses and saloons and wondered if coming to such a small town was the right thing to do.

There was no going back. She'd made her bed and would be lying in it whether she wanted to or not. She reached up and felt Adam's wedding ring on the gold chain around her neck.

*I hope I've made the right decision.*

# CHAPTER 3

They walked to the west end of the smallest town Alice had ever seen. The entire main street was only about four blocks long. The hotel, mercantile, and courthouse were the largest buildings and they weren't as big as most small buildings in New York. She was beginning to wonder if she'd made a terrible mistake, but she was determined to make the best of this marriage, this opportunity.

Alice picked up Melly just a block away from the courthouse and carried her. Doc's office appeared to be in the midst of the saloons and whorehouses of Hope's Crossing.

"Why is your office here rather than in a…uh…better part of town?"

"When I first came here, most of my patients came from this part of town. The miners and the girls who serve them were a lot of the clientele when I moved here. As the town is growing I have more patients who live on the other side of town, but most of them still are the miners and the girls they visit."

She nodded. "I understand. That makes sense. You also won't keep them from seeking treatment if you are really a part of their community. Hope's Crossing may be small, but I can already tell which parts of town are which."

It was easy to tell. All of the saloons and houses of ill repute were raw wood, whereas at the other end of town all of the businesses looked well-kept and like they had just been freshly painted. She suddenly realized she could actually see the other end of the town. This was definitely the smallest town she'd ever been in and she'd made it her home. *What was I thinking?*

At three stories the hotel was the tallest building in town and was painted pale yellow. The mercantile, immediately west, was bright green and definitely had fresh paint. The butcher shop on the west side of the mercantile was dark red. The other businesses clustered along the center of town on Main Street, included a newspaper, the sheriff's office, a bank, and gun smith.

They finally reached a large building painted white. The back half of the house was two-stories, but the front half was only one. The two-story portion appeared to have been added more recently.

"Here we are. Home sweet home."

Through the side door behind the front half of the building, they entered a large kitchen with a table for six on one wall, a four-burner stove and the stairway to the upper floor on another. To their left as they went in was a long counter with cupboards above and below, a sink in the middle with a small water pump and an icebox at the end. The wall directly to her right had a board, about six feet off the floor, with pegs nailed in it.

This was a nice kitchen. Much bigger than the one she'd had in New York.

Jeremiah hung his coat and she followed suit with her and Melly's coats.

"You could make some coffee if you would like. I'll take your bags up to the bedroom. You'll find the coffee in the smallest of the canisters next to the icebox."

She looked to where he pointed and saw

four ceramic canisters with colorful painted mushrooms.

"They are very nice."

"Payment for a birthing. The mother makes them to bring in a little extra money. Her husband is a miner."

"Do many families live here in Hope's Crossing?"

"A little less than fifty, but the number is getting larger every month."

"What is out there?" She pointed at the doorway on the same wall as the table.

"The front part of the house is my clinic. I'll show you as we go out to greet the patients. When I get back down we'll get started caring for them."

"Fine." This is another reason he doesn't get any rest. Doctors in New York don't live and work in the same building. She definitely must *insist* on having regular office hours.

While Jeremiah went upstairs, she lit the stove and put the coffee on to boil. She looked around and decided she liked this kitchen. It was big, airy and bright. With a few colorful towels and pot holders it would be about perfect. Alice knew she was expected to do the cooking and cleaning as well as all the duties of a nurse. It would be difficult to begin with, but she'd get used to it.

"What do you think, my darling?" She crouched down to Melly's height.

"I like Jemimah."

"It's Jeremiah. And why did you kick him if you like him?"

She shrugged. "Didn't like Jemimah then."

"Why do you like him now?"

"Don't know. Just do."

"I see."

Jeremiah chuckled as he entered the kitchen. "Why doesn't she just call me Doc, until she gets older? You said she's three? She's such a tiny little girl. Of course, you're not very big yourself. She's certainly got your eyes."

"It is a family trait...the violet eyes. Melly, can you say Doc?"

"Doc."

Alice pointed at Jeremiah. "This is Doc."

Melly smiled. "Hiya, Doc."

"Hello, Melly."

He bent and tickled her chin.

"You sure are a pretty little thing, just

like your mama."

Alice warmed all over at his words. She liked the fact that he didn't speak baby talk to her daughter.

"She's learning her numbers and her letters, too."

"I tree, see." She held up three fingers.

"That's very good. How old is your mama?"

Melly shook her head. "Old."

Alice's mouth dropped open.

Jeremiah roared with laughter.

"Your daughter is very smart, even though she has some problems with pronunciation. She knows what's what." He still chuckled but said, "I made room in the closet and the dresser for your clothes. The house has two bedrooms, so if you don't have enough room in our bedroom, use the closet and bureau in the other. I don't have a crib. Will Melly be all right in a regular bed?"

"Oh yes, she'll be fine and if I need to I'll use her closet. Thank you."

"You're welcome."

She turned away knowing she would be expected to perform the duties of a wife in the bedroom as well. She hadn't been with anyone since before Adam died. Though they'd loved each other very much, his work schedule didn't leave a lot of time for love making, which was why they only had one child. Her experience in the marriage bed didn't calm her unease about what would happen tonight.

Alice and Melly followed Jeremiah through the door to what would have been a hall to a parlor and found it opened to the back of his clinic. They walked up to the front, past two small treatment rooms and one surgery. Waiting for the doctor was a room full of about a dozen people.

Melly held her mother's hand and her dolly.

Alice would have her play area behind the desk out of the way. She saw a couple of young children among the patients. A play area for the kids was needed. She'd see about that later.

"Doc!" called a woman from across the room.

"Doc!" yelled a man.

The voices came from every direction, all wanting the doctor's immediate attention.

"Quiet," shouted Doc. "You all know that is not how the process works. I want to know who the first person here was."

A woman holding a small child raised her hand.

"That would be me, Doc. My Bertha is sick. She's hot and won't eat. Last night she threw up four times."

Jeremiah went over to the woman and plucked the listless child from her arms.

"Follow me," he said. "Alice, please triage the rest of the patients. The most critical I'll see first."

"Yes, Doctor." She turned to the room. "Ladies and gentlemen," she said loudly. "Please come up to the desk one at a time, starting with this man here." She pointed to her right. "I'll be asking your name and the problem you want to see the doctor about."

She listened and talked, wrote notes and put all the people in order of medical need.

"Alice," Jeremiah called from down the hall.

"Coming."

With a glance at Melly, who played quietly, she rushed down the hall to the examination room. The space was little more than a room with a table, covered by a sheet, a small cupboard with a drawer and a single chair. The mother occupied the chair and the little girl, who couldn't have been more than two, laid on the table on her side curled in the fetal position. She clearly wasn't feeling well.

"I need you to write Mrs. Johnson a note for peppermint to give to Lavernia Smith at the mercantile. There is a pad in the drawer," he inclined his head toward the cupboard. "Bertha here has an upset stomach."

"Yes, Doctor."

He turned to Mrs. Johnson.

"Hannah, you give the note Alice writes for you to Lavernia. She'll get you what you need and then you brew a couple of the leaves just like you would tea, let it cool and then have Bertha drink it. Do you understand?"

"Yes, Doc. Thank you."

The woman handed Jeremiah a dollar, took the child into her arms and left the room.

"Why did I just write that note for her?"

"Mrs. Johnson can't read or write and my handwriting is God awful. I thought Lavernia had a better shot at getting the child what she needs if you wrote it."

Alice was aware that everything she did

was being scrutinized by Jeremiah and tried very hard to be professional. She could diagnose most of these people as well as he could but she still had to be careful. She needed him to trust her.

"I understand. I've sorted out the folks up front. One is an elderly man who doesn't appear to have any symptoms but insists that he doesn't feel good. Unless you have a reason for me not to, I've put him last."

"Gray hair, wiry and holding a cane but not really using it?"

"That's him."

"He comes in about once a week. There is not a thing wrong with him, but he wants someone to talk to. Now that someone can be you rather than me, which is wonderful."

When Alice went back out to the front, she saw Melly talking to the old man.

"What's yer name, little one?"

"Melly. My daddy's a doctor."

"Is he now? That's very interesting." The old man rubbed his chin with his fingers. "How old are you?"

"Tree." She held up three fingers.

"Well now, I thought you just got here, but Doc must have been keeping you and your ma hid."

Alice walked up to them.

"I'm Alice Kilarney. This little darling," she put her hand on Melly's head, "is my daughter from my previous marriage, Melly Carter. My late husband, Melly's father, was also a doctor."

The man's shoulders fell and he sighed.

"Darn. I thought I had some juicy gossip."

She laughed. "I know you did. What's your name?"

"Walt Rogers, but just call me Walt."

"I'll be right back." She picked up the notes for the next patient. "Wilma Sanders."

A pretty dark skinned girl came forward. "I'm Wilma."

"Follow me, please."

When she returned, Alice sat in the chair next to Walt. "What do you do for a living Walt? Are you a miner?"

"I got me a little claim up yonder with a cabin on it and get enough gold to live on. Not a fortune, but I live just fine. Gets a little lonely up there all by my lonesome though."

"I bet it does."

She looked up and saw Doc signaling her.

"Excuse me, I'll be right back."

She hurried back to Doc, anxious she'd done something wrong. "Are you ready for another patient? I didn't see anyone leave."

"No, I need your help. Mrs. Sanders has a sick baby but won't let me take the child to examine it. Will you talk to her?"

"Certainly."

They walked to the examination room together.

Inside, sitting on the table in the middle of the room was the young Indian girl.

Alice went up to her. "Wilma?"

The girl looked up at her with huge dark eyes, terror written on her face.

"Is this your baby?"

Placing her hand on the baby's head, Alice felt the child's skin under the guise of a caress. The little one was hot, definitely had a fever.

"Can I see your baby?"

When Wilma balked and started shaking her head, she changed her tactic.

"You can hold him. Is the child a boy?"

Wilma nodded and unwrapped the baby.

"Oh, he's beautiful."

Alice scanned his body looking for hints that would tell her what was wrong with him. She was aware that Jeremiah watched her. Aware her life as a doctor hung in the balance, based on what he saw, his vision and his alone. *What if I make a mistake? Will I get Jeremiah killed like Adam was? I was there when Rebecca Lane passed away. There was nothing either of us could have done. Not Adam, not me. But what if...*

Her thoughts trailed off and she was back to business. *Nothing that happened before matters now. I was not responsible for Adam's death. I was not!*

"I see he's got a rash on his arms, may I lift his shirt and look at his belly?"

"Yes," said the girl.

Just as she feared, the child's torso was covered in spots. He had the measles. Now Melly would probably get them, too. It was a childhood sickness and she would be better of getting them now rather than later.

"What is your son's name?"

"Michael, after his father."

"Well, Michael has the measles. He'll be fine but he'll be uncomfortable for a while. No medicine is available for this disease. Give him lukewarm baths to help with the fever, be sure and keep him clean, change his diaper often and keep it dry as possible.

Can you do that?"

Wilma nodded. "Thank you, Mrs. Doc." Then she jumped down from the table.

"You're welcome."

The young woman walked over to Doc and placed something in his hand.

"Thank you, Wilma."

She nodded and walked out the door.

"What did she give you?"

Doc held up a string of bright blue stones.

"That's beautiful. Those look like sapphires."

"Might be. She makes them. I don't know where she gets the stones. She gave me a purple one that would look good with your eyes." He handed her the jewelry. "Here you have it."

Alice took the necklace and slipped it over her head.

"What do you think?"

"Lovely."

She cocked an eyebrow and smiled. "Why Jeremiah, if I didn't know better I'd think you were staring at my person with something other than benign interest."

His head snapped up. "Uh…wh…what? Oh…no. Just admiring the necklace. It looks…quite nice with your dress."

She looked down at her pink seersucker dress. The necklace did look lovely.

Alice fingered the stones. "Thank you, Jeremiah."

"You're welcome. Guess we'd better get the next patient in here."

"Uh, yes. I'll go. I need to check on Melly and Walt."

"Walt? Is he still here? I figured after he talked to you for a while he'd just go home."

"He's playing with Melly. You were right he's just lonely and she seems to like him."

"That's good. He'll leave me alone now."

Alice walked back out to the front. They'd seen two patients and four more had come in. That was the way it seemed to go all day long. She took time out at midday to prepare lunch for all of them, including Walt, who still played with Melly.

"You two come with me. It's time for lunch. I'll bring Jeremiah's back to him.

That gave Alice an idea.

In the kitchen, she took the sandwiches and coffee to the table. She gave Walt his and looked on as he and Melly played with her dolls. He seemed to be thoroughly enjoying himself and Melly loved having someone to play with.

"Walt, can I talk to you for a minute? Melly, eat your lunch, sweetheart."

"Sure. What can I do for you Mrs. Kilarney?"

"Are you enjoying yourself today, playing with Melly?"

"Oh, yes ma'am. She's a right smart little girl."

Alice smiled. "Yes, she is. What would you think about coming in everyday to play with her while I work with Doc? I'll feed you breakfast, lunch and if you want you can stay for dinner, too."

His eyes lit and then filled with tears.

"I can't think of anything I'd like more. Are you sure? You don't really know me."

"I'm a pretty good judge of character and Melly has had more fun today than she's had in a long time. Usually it's just her and me. I don't have the time to spend with her that I should and I know she gets lonely, being by herself most of the time. She's giggled more today than I've heard her since before her father died."

"I'm sorry for your loss. Was she close

to her daddy?"

"Very. She was the light in his life."

"Well if you're sure, I'd be plumb delighted. I'll work my claim in the mornings and on Saturday and Sunday. That should be enough for a little spending money. If I don't have to buy food, I don't need much money."

"Good. I appreciate your help." She looked down at her daughter. "What do you think about that, Melly? You want to play with Walt almost every day?'

Melly looked up at Walt and then down at her dolly. "Granpa Walt'll pay wif me all da time?"

"Grandpa?"

"I told her she could call me Grandpa Walt. I hope that's okay."

"That's great." Alice turned to Melly. "That's right, sweetie. What do you think? Would you like that?"

Melly looked at Walt and beamed.

"Yup."

"All right then. We have an agreement. Let's eat."

Jeremiah walked in from the clinic, unrolling his sleeves and buttoning the cuffs as he did.

"Is there something I should know?"

*****

Dick Lane was a man on the run. He had killed the doctor who murdered his wife, but he still had one more person to kill. Alice Carter. The doctor's wife. Why should she live when his beautiful Rebecca died. It wasn't fair, but soon all would be done. Just the woman. He wouldn't kill her child. The little girl would survive. After all he wasn't a monster.

He'd tried to kill Alice in New York but she almost never left the house. The one time she did, he followed her and stole a carriage to run her down but a man pulled her out of the way.

The old lady next door to her was a font of information even if she didn't know it. That was how he found out she was leaving New York and he followed her from the big city to this out of the way place. Hope's Crossing, Montana Territory. Why would she come here? He listened to the saloon gossip and it wasn't long before he knew. She was starting a new life as another doctor's wife. Why should his family, his world, be destroyed while she has the chance to start a new one? Well, she wouldn't have this new family for long.

Too bad…for the new doctor. Looked like he would soon be a widower.

For now, Dick was holed up in this hovel above the Branch Water saloon. He'd changed his hair from blond to black and dyed his beard black, too. The woman whose room it was, didn't ask questions. She worked at night and then Dick had to vacate the premises. But the rest of the time he could slake his lust on the woman and plan his revenge at the same time.

# CHAPTER 4

"What did you do with the patients?" asked Alice

"I told them I'd be back in about half an hour."

"Good. I'm glad you're taking time out to eat."

"You're not answering my question. What should I know?"

She cocked her head.

"Just that Walt will be watching Melly for me so we can work. I've told him I'll provide him all meals if he would do that. He's agreed. Do you want to say something?"

He looked over at Walt, who was look at him with anxious eyes. She saw the fear that Jeremiah would say no.

"I'd say we're getting the better part of the deal. Welcome to the family, Walt."

*****

At six o'clock Alice took the sign she'd made, pinned it to the screen door and locked the wooden door. No more patients today.    Doc—Jeremiah—would    have working hours whether he wanted them or not.

She walked to where Walt and Melly played. Melly was so tired but she was still her sweet self. She didn't get a nap today. That couldn't happen again. She needed her nap.

"Well how did your day go you two?"

She looked down at the drawing they were coloring. The crayons were a gift from Adam's great-aunt Tilly in England. Alice had been unable to find them for purchase in America. The drawing was of Melly.

"Walt, you never said anything about being an artist."

"You never asked. 'Sides, it's not something I bandy about much."

Jeremiah walked over after letting the last patient out and relocking the door.

"I didn't think I would, but I like the sign and the locked door. I want to be able to spend time with my new family. And Walt, you never talk about being an artist. No one in town knows you can draw like that. Come on family. Let's go see what's for dinner. You, too, Walt."

When they got to the kitchen, Alice opened the icebox and saw they needed to go to the market.

"Looks like you're buying us dinner tonight, Jeremiah. You have enough eggs and bacon for breakfast tomorrow, but that's it."

"All right, let's head to the hotel and get supper. That's what I usually do anyway unless someone pays for their visit with food. Normally, I would have gotten a chicken or two from someone today."

"How much did you collect today? I collected five dollars and this beautiful necklace."

"I've got another ten and ten more on account. How did you like your first day?" asked Jeremiah.

They walked outside and there was a chill in the air. Alice buttoned her coat and made sure Melly's was buttoned as well.

"I loved it. I was able to help you and the patients at the same time. I think I saw as many people as you did. If you'd been alone you would still be there."

"That's true. This is the first time in a

long while that I've eaten supper at a normal hour. Thank you, Alice."

"You're welcome."

"What about you Walt?" asked Alice. "Still want to come and watch Melly every day? If you don't, I understand."

"Oh, yes, ma'am. Me and this little nugget," he ruffled Melly's hair. "Well, we seemed to have a good time. She learned to play checkers today. I still have to remind her when to go, but she can see how and where to jump. I can't believe she's only three."

"I almost four." Melly shed her mother's hand and held up four fingers. Then she took Alice's hand again.

Alice smiled. "She knows her numbers and her letters, I'm teaching her how to read now."

Jeremiah looked down at Melly. "My goodness, she really is advanced for her age."

"She is. I think she'll keep Walt on his toes."

Walt chuckled.

"You're right about that. If the weather's nice tomorrow, I thought we could play in the yard or take a walk to the mercantile."

He leaned over and whispered to Alice, "They got a whole new batch of penny candy."

Alice laughed. "You'll spoil her."

Walt grinned. "She deserves a little spoilin'."

"Mama, what's spoilin'?"

"It just means making you happy."

Melly nodded her little head, her blonde curls bouncing in the late day sun.

"I like bein' happy."

Alice patted her daughter's hand.

"I like for you to be happy, too."

Jeremiah opened the door to the hotel and held it for everyone.

"Here we are."

"Doc, who are the newcomers?" asked Jesse Donovan, there with his wife Clare.

"This is my wife, Alice and her daughter Melly, and our friend Walt here I think you know. Alice, these nice people are Jesse and Clare Donovan. Jesse is one of the mine owners."

The tall, dark haired man held the hand of a pretty woman with curly red hair.

"Pleased to meet you Mrs. Kilarney," said Jesse.

"Oh, no please, call me Alice."

"Certainly. And we're Jesse and Clare. We'll have to see about having a party to welcome you to Hope's Crossing," said Jesse.

"That's not necessary, but would be very nice," said Alice.

"We'll let you know when it will be."

"Thank you. It was very nice to meet you both."

"And you," said Jesse.

"Yes, it's wonderful to have another woman in town. We are gaining but are still out numbered ninety to one."

"My goodness. That's staggering to me." Alice put her hand to her throat.

Clare nodded. "Women are a rare commodity here."

"So I see."

"Come Clare, let's let them eat their dinner. It looks like Effie is bringing it now."

Alice looked to where Jesse was and saw Effie carrying four plates of steaming food.

"See you soon," said Clare.

"We will. Thank you," said Alice

"Goodnight, Jesse, Clare." Doc dipped his head at Clare.

After a wonderful meal, they left the building and walked back home. It was dark when they left. Walt carried Melly and Alice held Jeremiah's arm.

"There are so many stars here. I have never seen so many."

"That's because we don't have all the lights that New York does."

"That's true."

They reached the house and Alice turned to Walt. "See you tomorrow? Seven o'clock for breakfast."

"I'll be here."

Walt headed west to his cabin while they went inside their home.

"I tired, Mama."

Alice picked up Melly.

"I bet you are, baby. You were such a good girl today. Do you like playing with Walt?"

"Yup. He's fun. Kinda like Granpa."

She laid her head on Alice's shoulder.

"He is isn't he? I knew he reminded me of someone. Do you miss Grandpa, sweetie?"

She nodded.

"And Daddy, too."

A pang of pain flashed through Alice as

she thought of Adam. She missed him, too. More than anyone knew. She did her best not to let it show, refusing to break down in front of anyone. Up until now, she'd been able to cry in her bed, away from Melly, but she couldn't do that tonight. Tonight she was another man's wife and expected to perform as one.

She reached up and fingered the ring on a chain around her neck. Adam's ring. She refused to take it off, except perhaps when she and Jeremiah were making love. The rest of the time she would wear it and if he didn't like it, that was just too bad.

"I know." She turned to Jeremiah, "I'm putting Melly down and then I'll be back. Would you put on the kettle to heat? We can have some tea."

"All right. See you in a bit."

Alice walked upstairs to the spare bedroom, which she recognized because her valises were *not* in the room. She sat Melly on the bed and took off her shoes and socks.

"You wait right here while I go get your nightgown."

She went across the hall, to retrieve Melly's valise from Jeremiah's bedroom.

From the luggage she put all the

garments on the bed until she found Melly's night-clothes. The flannel gown was a little big on her, but she'd grow into—and then out of—it in no time. Alice took off the rest of Melly's clothes and then pulled the nightgown over her head.

"There you go."

Melly's room was simply furnished. One light wood nightstand was beside the iron bed. Across the room from the bed was the closet door. On the same wall as the door to the hall stood a dresser and directly across the room from the dresser was a window covered with red gingham curtains.

On the bed lay a beautiful patchwork quilt. As Alice turned down the covers she saw a plain brown wool blanket between the sheet and the quilt. Melly should be plenty warm.

Her baby crawled onto the bed.

Alice covered her bringing the blankets up to just under her chin.

"Do you want a story tonight?"

"Yup. Pease."

Alice reached into the very bottom of the valise and brought out a large book full of children's stories.

"Okay, how about *The Three Little*

*Pigs*?"

Melly nodded and scooted closer to Alice until she could put her head in her mother's lap.

"Once upon a time…"

Twenty minutes later…

"The end."

Alice gazed down at her daughter's face. Her violet eyes were closed and she slept soundly. Alice lifted Melly's head and scooted out from under it.

"Does she always go to sleep so easily?"

Alice gasped, her hand flying to her throat.

"Jeremiah!"

"I'm sorry. I didn't mean to startle you."

She picked up the lamp from the nightstand, moved toward him and out into the hall.

"To answer your question, yes, she usually goes to sleep easily. Tonight even quicker than normal. She didn't get a nap today. Tomorrow, I'm asking Walt to bring her up to her room to take a nap in the afternoon. She's used to getting two naps a day, but one will do."

He frowned. "If she needs two, then just ask him to bring her in the morning and after lunch. I'm sure he'd be happy to take a snooze himself. That was a good idea asking him to play with her. The situation will be good for them both."

She nodded. "I thought so. She told me tonight she misses her grandpa and her daddy."

"I imagine she does. You probably miss him, her father, too."

Her back stiffened. They stood in the hall outside Jeremiah's bedroom.

"Yes, I do. Very much, but that doesn't mean I won't be a good wife to you. I will. I know my duty."

"I don't want your duty. I want you to want me as much as I desire you. I know that will take a while, therefore, I propose that for this first week or so you sleep with Melly. We'll get to know each other a bit and then go to the next step of our marriage."

Alice felt a tear roll down her cheek.

"You would do that?"

"I'm not an unreasonable man. I'd like us to get this marriage off on the right foot, so to speak."

"I'd like that, too."

"I'll bring your bag in here, and then we

can enjoy a quiet cup of tea."

"Thank you, Jeremiah. You don't know how much this gesture means to me."

He flushed and ran his hand behind his neck.

"You're welcome. I…um…I'll meet you in the kitchen."

He turned and headed to his bedroom.

She smiled and walked downstairs to the kitchen where the kettle whistled. She went to the stove and took it off the burner. Alice looked around the kitchen for the tea leaves and cups, opening and closing cupboards making mental notes of what was where, until she found the items she needed.

She measured out the leaves into the cups and poured the hot water over them to steep.

Jeremiah came in and sat at the table.

Alice brought the cups and sat with him.

"Tell me about yourself. For instance," she jutted her chin toward his cup. "Do you take milk, lemon or sugar in your tea?"

"No. Just the tea. Take my coffee black, too."

"I noticed that at dinner. I take mine with cream and sugar, when it's available, which it hasn't been for us of late. What made a doctor like you take up residence in this little town? You couldn't have been a prospector…were you?"

He grinned at her.

"No, not a prospector."

He closed both hands around the mug of coffee. *I had too much pain to stay any one place. Susan drove all caring out of me. Drove all love out of me.*

"After the War Between the States ended, the house and girl I left, were both gone when I came home. I wandered from place to place, never really finding a anywhere I wanted to stay. When I hit Hope's Crossing, I discovered so much need and they had no doctor. There were a couple of women, wives of miners, who did their best to treat injuries, but situations arose which they couldn't deal with. People died needlessly."

Alice placed her hand on top of his. "I'm sorry for your loss."

He didn't shake her off.

"What about you? I know you're a widow, but that's about all."

She brought back her hand and wrapped both around her cup as he had done, suddenly needing the warmth. "My husband was a doctor as well. Well-respected surgeon, Adam Carter. Perhaps you heard of him?"

Jeremiah shook his head. "No. I'm sorry. We don't get a lot of news up here."

She spoke slowly, quietly, closed her eyes against the pain of memories."After Adam was murdered—"

"Wait, stop."

He reached for her hand.

She pulled it out of his reach.

He didn't try again, realizing she needed the separation right now. She returned her hand to the cup.

"Your husband was murdered? Why?"

"The police think it was because he lost a patient in surgery. Her husband blamed Adam and shot him in the back one night as he left the hospital. At least that's the theory the police are working from. They never caught the person who did it. For a long time, I was afraid the perpetrator would come after me and Melly, but he didn't. At least that I know of."

"Now, I'm the one who's sorry. I can't imagine what you must have gone through. When did this happen?"

"Six months ago."

"Alice, you're not even out of mourning yet." He reached his hand so he could squeeze hers and she let him.

"I've had to be. Mourning is for people who can afford it. I was running out of money and no one in New York would hire me, so I became a mail-order bride. I don't regret my choice. This was one of the most fulfilling days I've had in a long time. Thank you for that." She smiled and then sipped her tea.

"You're welcome. I never expected my bride to be a doctor. I admit the idea takes some getting used to, but I watched you today with some of the patients you treated. You made the same diagnosis that I would have. Every time."

Her chest warmed with pride. "I'm glad you confirmed my work. If you'd disagreed I'm sure you would have said something."

"I most definitely would have and I would have told you to stop treating the patients. But you were very good with them. Not that I'm ready to have you working as a doctor, I still want your duties, at least for now, to be mostly a nurses duties."

Alice pulled back her hand. She thought she'd made headway but he still didn't trust her to do what she was trained for. She'd just have to work harder for his approval for she intended to get it and to work beside her husband in equal capacity.

"I think I best get to bed. Melly always wakes up early. Do you have any oatmeal?"

"There might be some in the lower cupboard next to the icebox."

She walked to the counter and searched the cupboard for the cereal, finding the unopened box way in the back.

"If we don't get more eggs tomorrow, we'll all be having oatmeal for breakfast the day after that. Of course, that is not such a bad thing and something we will do to vary our diet."

"I hear you. I have an account at the mercantile. Tomorrow why don't you go with Walt and Melly and pick up whatever you need. I'm surprised you found that." He pointed at the box of oats.

"So was I and thank you. I will go to the mercantile tomorrow. I'm anxious to see more of the town and meet more people. I need them to like and trust me in order for me to treat them."

# CHAPTER 5

They left the clinic in the fog. Cold air had moved in overnight and the sun hadn't burned off the fog by the time they left for grocery shopping.

Alice was very glad Walt came with her to the mercantile. By the time she'd picked up the necessities from there and gone to the butchers, there would be much too much for her to carry back by herself.

A bell sounded as they entered the store.

"Be right there," said a high feminine voice.

After a moment or two, a tiny woman came around the corner. She had to be the smallest person Alice had ever seen next to the woman she'd met last night. As a matter of fact, Effie looked an awful lot like this woman. Both of them made Alice, at five feet two inches, feel like a veritable giant.

"Well, hello there, Walt. Who you got with you?"

Walt pointed at Alice and Melly. "This here is Doc's new wife, Alice, and her little one, Melly. They come to stock Doc's cupboards."

The little woman turned to Alice and held out her hand. "Pleased to meet you. Name's Lavernia Smith. I own this mercantile. What all do you need today?"

Alice shook the woman's hand. "Pleased to meet you, Lavernia. I've discovered Jeremiah needs just about everything, flour, sugar, butter, milk, all the basics."

"I'm not surprised. Why, Doc hardly cooks anything. I usually see him at dinner time in the restaurant my sister runs." She looked down a Melly. "You sure are a pretty one. Look just like your mama. Would you like a stick of candy?"

"Yup." She looked up at her mother. "Can I Mama? Huh? Pease?"

"All right," said Alice before turning back to Lavernia. "That's where I thought I saw you. You and your sister could be twins."

"We are." Lavernia laughed. "Her name is Iphigenia but everyone calls her Effie. She says I'm older but she really is. Don't tell her I said that. She'll just get in a huff and insist it's the other way around." She handed Melly an orange stick of candy. "Here you go sweetie."

"Tank you." Melly took the stick and happily put it in her mouth.

Alice laughed. "You definitely sound like sisters."

She pulled the piece of paper from her reticule and handed it to Lavernia. "I made a list of the foodstuffs we need. Jeremiah said he has an account here." *What if he doesn't have enough credit to cover all the things I put on the list. What can we do without?*

Lavernia looked it over. "Oh, he does. Anything the doc wants goes on his account. We tally up at the end of the month. Do you want to wait for this or come back later?"

"We'll wait. Walt will help carry the groceries home for me. Or do you think we should come back with the buggy"

"It shouldn't take too long to put this together. You shouldn't need the buggy. I'll put it all in a sturdy box and only give you enough for a week. If you want more flour or anything else in great quantity, you might want to bring the buggy."

Alice made a mental note to bring the buggy next time.

"Actually, now that I think on it, we'll go next door to the butcher and get our meat for the week."

"I should have this ready when you come back"

"Thank you. We'll return shortly."

Alice, Walt and Melly went to the butcher and Alice chose a beef roast, pork roast, two chickens, two pounds of bacon and one pound of sausage. The butcher wrapped it all in paper and put the packages in a burlap bag to carry them home.

When they got back to the mercantile, Lavernia was putting the last item in a box.

"I got everything on your list except the cinnamon. I'll have to order that. It'll be here in about a month. I boxed your groceries so Walt can carry them for you."

"Thank you, Lavernia. I appreciate it."

"Yes ma'am. It's all taken care of."

"See you again soon." Alice bent down and looked at her daughter. "What do you say to Miss Smith?"

Melly took the orange stick out of her mouth. "G'bye, Miss Smiff. Tank you for da candy."

The old lady chuckled.

"You're welcome, sweetie. You come see old Lavernia any time."

Alice, Walt and Melly walked back to the house. Alice hurried to put all the food and meat away before going into the clinic. She was anxious to get to her real work. Walt and Melly were already there, playing checkers in the corner of the waiting room.

"All right," said Alice to the patients waiting. "Who's next?"

\*\*\*\*\*

Two weeks had passed and though Jeremiah hadn't mentioned her sleeping in his bed again, Alice knew she was on borrowed time. Rather than put all the pressure on him to make the change, she would talk to him. The time had arrived. Time for them to begin being a real family. Time for Melly to sleep by herself.

After breakfast and after Walt had taken Melly to the clinic to play, she approached him. "Jeremiah, I'd like to talk to you if you have time."

"Certainly."

He brought his coffee cup to the sink where she stood.

"I want to talk to you about something

as well."

She stood with her back to the sink. "What did you want to discuss."

"Ladies first."

She nodded, took a deep breath, and squared her shoulders. "I want to move to our bedroom. Melly is old enough to sleep alone and the time has come that we consummated this marriage."

He smiled. "I wanted to talk to you about the same thing and with the same thought."

Her stance eased.

"Would tonight be too soon?"

"I think tonight would be fine."

"I'll move my things after dinner. Perhaps you can read Melly her story tonight."

"I'd be pleased to read to her. I think she and I need to become better acquainted. At some point, when she is ready, I'd like for her to think of me as her father."

"I think that would be wonderful. I don't want her to ever forget her father, but I want her to see you, and refer to you, as her parent. She's young enough, she won't remember her daddy for much longer, but I'll help her to recall him. I think she needs to."

"I understand and agree that would be best. I never thought I'd be a father and yet someday, I hope she'll call me Daddy."

"As do I."

Jeremiah took Alice's hands in his. "There is something I've been wanting to do for some time now."

He pulled her closer and wrapped his arms around her, then he lowered his head and placed his lips against hers.

The kiss was a heady thing. At first gentle and soft, then he pressed his tongue against her lips, asking for entry.

She granted it, and the kiss changed. He explored her, and she dueled with him. Wrapping her arms around his neck she pulled her body flush with his. She felt his ardor pressing against her stomach.

He broke the kiss and looked down at her, his mouth turned up in a half smile.

"Today will be too long, knowing that you wait for me at the end."

Alice lowered her gaze to the floor. It was a exhilarating feeling knowing that her husband wanted her. She was delighted and a little frightened, too. The only man she had ever been with was Adam, her late husband.

What if Jeremiah expected her to know things that she didn't? Would he teach her? She and Adam had learned together. Would that be enough?

They parted and went their separate ways to prepare for the day.

Alice had fashioned a small play area for children in the waiting room. She put a braided rug under the small wooden table she'd had Walt make. They pulled chairs up to it, so they weren't sitting on the floor playing.

Melly and Walt spent part of their days there, coloring the drawings that Walt made, playing checkers or playing dolls. The sight of that grown man playing dolls with her precious daughter always brought a smile. When other children came in, Melly talked to them and shared her crayons.

Although Alice worried about Melly being exposed to all the germs that the children might bring, she thought it was no different than if she were in school. Alice was of the opinion that it was better for her to get the childhood diseases over and done with. She would build her immunities up this way as well.

She also was cautious and only had them

in the play area for the morning. After Melly's first nap they stayed at the house and played or read or went for a walk. Walt kept her busy with lots of activities. He was even teaching her how to draw.

On one of their forays to the mercantile Walt bought a set of jacks, and they were both learning how to play the game. Finally, Alice took pity on them and showed the pair how to play. Alice loved to hear Melly's peals of laughter when she picked up the jacks and caught the ball.

When the weather was nice Walt took Melly outside and taught her about the local plants and animals.

"Mama, guess what?"

Alice was between patients and so could give Melly her full attention.

"What?"

"Granpa Walt and me went to the crick."

Alice looked up at Walt, a bit alarmed.

"Don't worry," said Walt. "I was always between her and the water."

Alice let out a breath. "Thank God."

A patient came in and put their name down then sat.

"Melly, I have to go to work now. You can tell me about your trip later."

She watched her precious daughter's shoulders slump as she nodded and went back to Walt.

Those were the times that Alice wished she didn't have such a calling to medicine. The fact that she couldn't concentrate on Melly worried Alice's heart. She wanted to be able to drop everything and listen to whatever Melly had to tell her but she couldn't. She had responsibilities, work to do. Instead, she watched her precious baby turn away, with her shoulders slumped, and go back to Walt.

Alice closed her eyes, promising herself she'd spend more time with her daughter in the evenings. But hadn't she just told Jeremiah that he could read to Melly tonight? Was there any reason they both couldn't be in the room with her while she went to sleep? Absolutely not. All three of them…together…was the right solution to this particular problem, but still didn't absolve her of the guilt she felt for working.

At precisely six o'clock, Alice put the 'closed except for emergencies' sign on the door and locked it. Since she'd limited Jeremiah's hours and ensured he ate three meals a day, he'd started putting on weight.

He was no longer thin, but now was just lean. His face didn't seem as gaunt, and he actually looked younger with some weight on his bones.

In the morning she'd fixed a stew and let it simmer all day for supper that evening. Walt checked it for her at several times during the day and stirred the pot or added wood to the stove or water to the stew.

She'd baked bread the night before and had a pie they'd received that day in payment for Jeremiah's services.

Walt was now a part of their family. He dug his gold on Saturday and Sunday, and he still lived in his cabin, but he was at Jeremiah's for breakfast, lunch and dinner every day of the week. Alice liked having him there. She knew that Melly was safe with him.

"That was a good meal, Alice. You're a right fine cook." Walt patted his belly. "I think the doc here, and me, too, got real lucky when you answered his letter."

"Thank you. That's very kind of you to say."

"Only speakin' the truth."

Walt put his napkin on the table, stood and began gathering the dishes to take to the sink.

Alice had put a pot of water on to heat when they sat to eat. Now the water was hot and ready to do dishes. Usually Walt washed, Jeremiah dried and put the dishes away, while Alice got Melly ready for bed.

Neither man would admit to actually doing the dishes to anyone, but Walt did say it was nice to get his hands really clean once in a while, like when he washed the pots and pans.

Jeremiah did them because he was used to the chore and Alice needed the time with Melly. That he realized this need was definitely something she had not expected from a bachelor, doctor or not.

"Melly is ready for you both to say goodnight."

Alice stood in the doorway to the kitchen holding her daughter's hand.

Jeremiah handed Walt the towel to dry his hands and then they both came to the little girl.

"Good night, sweet thing. See you tomorrow," said Walt.

"G'night Grampa Walt."

Melly let go of her mother's hand, ran to Walt, hugged him and kissed his cheek.

He blushed and hugged her back.

"G'night, Jermimah."

Walt chuckled.

Jeremiah frowned at Walt, who had the good grace to look chastised.

"What did we say you would call me for now?"

"Doc. G'night, Doc."

"Goodnight, Melly," said Jeremiah. "I'll be up to read to you in a little while."

"'kay."

She turned and skipped down the hall to the staircase.

Alice walked over to Walt and kissed him on the cheek. "Goodnight, Walt. Be careful going home. Thanks for being my daughter's grandpa."

"Ah, now, it ain't nothin'. Anything for the little miss. See you tomorrow."

He ambled out the door.

Alice turned toward Jeremiah. "I thought if you don't mind, I'll sit in with you when you read to Melly tonight."

"Since this is my first time, that's probably a good idea. So she'll get used to me and know that it really is bedtime when I read a story, too."

"Thank you. For not having any children

of your own, you seem to understand them quite well and realize they need routine. The repetition makes them feel safe."

Jeremiah chuckled. "I get a lot of children acting up when they come in and think they don't have to mind me or their parents because they are sick. We get that idea right out of their little heads immediately. I don't allow them not to obey their parents."

They walked together to Melly's room.

She'd already gotten the Grimm's Fairy Tales book down from the shelf and crawled under the covers.

"Are you ready to hear more of your stories?"

She nodded vigorously. "Yup."

"Where did you leave off?" asked Jeremiah as he sat in the chair by the bed.

"We had just finished *Little Red Riding Hood*," said Alice.

"Let's see what the next story is." Jeremiah picked up the book and opened it to where the bookmark was tucked in the pages. "It looks like the next one is *Cinderella*. How does that sound, sweetheart?"

"Good."

Jeremiah began to read.

About five minutes later, Alice laid her hand on Jeremiah's arm and jutted her chin toward her sleeping daughter.

Jeremiah moved the bookmark to the new location and closed the book, setting it on the nightstand.

He stood, took Alice's hand and led her to their bedroom.

Alice took his hand with excitement and trepidation. She couldn't help but wonder if she would be comparing him to Adam or he would compare her to some other woman.

What if she couldn't perform the way he thought she should. What will he do?

With a sigh and a deep breath she entered their bedroom for the first night with her husband.

# CHAPTER 6

Normally they would have stayed up, reading, doing needlework or just talking about their day. But this wasn't any day. This was the same as their wedding night, since they hadn't had one before. Alice entered the bedroom followed by Jeremiah who closed the door after them.

"Are you nervous?"

His deep baritone sent shivers over her skin or was it that the room was cold? She didn't know which. All she knew for sure was she felt like a school girl on her wedding night.

"I am…a little."

"We're even. I'm nervous, too."

He took her hand in his. "You have beautiful hands. Strong and gentle at the same time."

"Th…thank you."

Jeremiah pulled her close. He took her face between his palms and lowered his head, meeting her halfway. Gently he closed his lips over hers.

She sighed and he slipped inside.

Anticipation made her eager. She met his thrusts of his tongue with her own. They tested and tasted one another; their tongues dueled neither one gaining superiority, each holding its own against the other.

Jeremiah's arms wrapped around her and brought her closer. Encasing her in his strength, he held her tight.

He broke the kiss and rested his forehead against hers.

"I want you so much. Since I first saw you, I've wanted you."

"You have me."

"I'm nervous. You have more experience making love than I do. At least more recent experience."

"I'm glad to hear that you haven't partaken of the wears of some of your clients."

"You're right. I don't visit the prostitutes. Tending them as I do doesn't give way to romantic notions."

"And do you have romantic notions now?"

He barked with laughter. "Oh, boy, howdy. Do I ever!"

She laughed.

He grinned.

Alice began to undo the buttons down her front of her blouse and then stopped, looking up at Jeremiah.

"Do you want me to undress?"

"Yes. I think we should both undress…now."

Stalling, she continued with her buttons, opened the shirtwaist and removed it, carefully hanging it on one of the pegs. She followed with her skirt and petticoat.

Now she only wore her corset, chemise, stockings and bloomers. She looked over at Jeremiah, gratified by the hunger she saw on his face as he watched her. She removed her corset and set it on the bureau. Her chemise and bloomers soon followed. Standing with her back to her husband, she slowly glanced over her shoulder at him.

He still watched her but had finished undressing and now lay on the bed atop the covers with his hands behind his head. He patted the mattress beside him.

"Don't be afraid of me Alice. I'm just a man like any other."

She nodded, but no words followed. Leaning over, she removed her stockings, rolling each one down her leg and off her foot. Then she hurried to the bed and tried to crawl under the covers.

Jeremiah waved his finger at her. "No blankets. Not yet."

She nodded and lay on her back.

He leaned toward her on the double iron bed and kissed the side of her neck.

The touch of his lips was warm, yet she shivered with excitement.

"Are you cold?" he whispered as though afraid to wake Melly.

"No. Just nervous."

"Don't be. I don't want to hurt you. If I do anything that you don't like or want, tell me. Having relations should be pleasurable for both husband and wife."

He reached up and touched her dead husband's wedding ring that she wore on a chain around her neck.

"Sit up, please."

He climbed out and came around to her side of the bed.

She looked up at him.

Jeremiah lifted the necklace with the ring over her head and off. He held the jewelry up, letting it dangle from his hand.

"You belong to me now."

He put the chain on her nightstand.

Irritation coursed through her. How dare he tell her she couldn't wear the ring? Yet he'd not taken it from her in anger. He didn't rip it from her. Instead he gently took the necklace off her and set it on the nightstand. Still she wasn't ready to set Adam aside. She loved him and just because he was dead, didn't mean she loved him any less. Later. She'd put the jewelry on again later and just make sure she had it off before they had relations, so he didn't see it again.

After walking around the bed and he crawled back to her.

"Now where were we? Ah, yes. I remember. Would you lie back, please? I feel the need to kiss you."

Still irritated, she did as he requested, lying flat on her back, her hands at her sides, stiff as a board.

He kissed her lips, long and deep.

She relaxed some.

Playing with an escaped tendril of hair, he kissed her neck, followed by little nips, soothed by the swipe of his tongue.

Sinking lower in the mattress, she sighed.

When he kissed his way down to her breast she was completely relaxed and able to enjoy his ministrations.

"That's better. I know you have passion in you, Alice. I intend to bring it out."

Jeremiah made his way down to her mons where he put his mouth on her and did things that Adam had never done. Made her feel things she'd never felt before. Made her shatter and scatter among the stars. He stayed with her, soothing her until she relaxed.

"Well, how did you like that?"

"Never...I...the feelings I experienced...amazing."

Jeremiah chuckled and then furrowed his brows. "Your husband never brought you to orgasm?"

She shook her head. "He and I were both virgins when we married. What little we knew we practiced our whole marriage. We didn't try new things."

"My darling, Alice. You have many wonderful things to learn about the play and satisfaction that can be had in the marriage bed. Now it's my turn."

He moved over her, covered her, loved her, and touched her bringing her to orgasm and then he soon followed.

"Oh, my God, Jeremiah," she panted, barely able to speak. "I don't think I could live through that again. It's too much pleasure."

"But you will. The night is young and since you were not a virgin, we have no need to wait, except for me to recuperate."

He pulled her to him and spooned with her while he 'recovered". There he fell asleep.

So did she, only to be awakened in the middle of the night with Jeremiah suckling her breast.

"I thought this might wake you up…or give you a really good dream."

"Or both." She placed both hands on his head and pressed it down toward her hungry flesh.

They had relations again, several times during the night, with naps in-between. By morning both were spent and only slightly rested.

Still lying in bed, she shifted to her side and watched her husband.

"Today will be a hard day. We've had so little sleep. Tonight we must do more sleeping."

He turned over and kissed her soundly.

"Yes, ma'am. I simply couldn't get enough of my beautiful wife. You are you know."

"What?"

"Beautiful."

She felt the heat rise and knew her cheeks must be flaming. "That's very kind of you to say."

"Nothing kind about telling the truth. Shall we dress for the day?"

She followed his gaze toward the window. There was no light showing but the rooster that awakened them was still crowing his head off.

"Why is that rooster crowing? There are hours before sunrise."

"The rooster is a menace to getting sleep. It crows at odd hours of the day and night. Melly has got to be wondering where her mother is. Do you want to check on her?"

"I told her I would be right across the hall. She'll be fine." *Then why was I worried about Melly spending her first night alone?*

He reached for her. "If you're sure…"

"I am. She would be knocking on the door—"

As if on cue there was an urgent rapping sounded on the door.

"Mama. Mama."

Alice hurried out of bed, grabbed her wrapper, and went to the door. She opened it wide.

Melly burst into the room.

"I had a bad dream." Tears ran down her beautiful little face.

Alice bent and opened her arms.

Melly ran into them. She cried, sniffled and cried some more.

"Would you like to sleep with Mama and Doc?"

Melly nodded, making her curls bounce.

Jeremiah sat upright.

"That's not wise, Alice."

Alice smoothed her hand over Melly's back.

"It will be fine. You just stay under the sheet and the blankets. I'll put her on top of the sheet under the blankets and I'll sleep between you."

He lifted his eyebrows and sighed.

"All right, if you say so. Wouldn't it just

be easier if you took her back to her bed and lay with her until she's asleep again?"

*Now he wants me to sleep with her?* "Well, yes, but I just thought you didn't want me sleeping with her anymore."

"When she's upset from a nightmare is different than sleeping the entire night with her. I'm sure her nightmares will subside once she gets used to sleeping alone."

Alice looked at her daughter and thought about what Jeremiah said. He was probably right.

"What was your dream about, sweetheart? Come with Mama back to your bed."

"You gonna sleep with me? The monsters won't get me?"

"No, the monsters won't get you." She turned to her husband. "I'll be back after she goes to sleep."

He smiled. "I'll be waiting."

She laughed. "You'll be sleeping and I'll probably fall asleep, too."

"Then I'll see you when you come back in a couple of hours to dress for the day."

Alice nodded and picked up Melly.

"Say goodnight to Doc."

Melly laid her head on her mother's

shoulder. "G'night, Doc."

"She's almost asleep now. You'd better go."

"See you in the morning. Goodnight."

Alice carried Melly back to her bed. Doc had been right. Melly was asleep before Alice laid her on the bed. She got in beside her daughter and pulled the covers over them both.

*You've got to get used to sleeping without me. I've been a bad mother, having you in bed with me since your father died. I've given us both bad habits. But now we need to form new habits. I need to sleep with my husband and you need to sleep alone. You won't like it but learning to be in our own bed is the right thing to do, both for my marriage and for your growth.*

Alice let those thoughts linger as she closed her eyes.

*****

Someone was rubbing her arm and it felt so good.

"Alice."

The voice whispered her name.

"Alice. Wake up, sweetheart."

Sweetheart? Adam?

No. Adam was dead.

*Jeremiah!*

"What? I'm late." She sat straight up in bed.

"Calm down." He pressed a hand to her shoulder. "You're fine, but it is time to get up. No hurry. I'll put on the coffee."

Alice gave a long exhale and rose from the bed. She felt like she'd just fallen asleep a moment before rather than two hours ago. Turning, she checked to make sure Melly was still covered, and then left to get dressed.

She donned a lavender dress that buttoned down the front. White lace edged the collar and the cuffs. The garment, though plain, made her eyes look even more purple than usual.

After she was dressed Alice made the bed. When she was straightening her side, she saw the chain with Adam's ring lying on her nightstand where Jeremiah had put it. She fingered the necklace. *Jeremiah has no right to tell me I can't wear this.* With that thought she dropped the gold chain over her head and tucked the ring under her dress. She'd have to remember to take the necklace off before he saw it when she undressed, but she *would* wear it.

She gathered her hair into a long plait and then pinned it in a coil on top of her head. Turning to the mirror over the dresser, she examined her reflection, decided it would do and headed to the kitchen.

Jeremiah sat at the table with a cup of coffee in his hand, reading yesterday's newspaper.

"Good morning."

She grabbed two skillets from where they hung on the wall behind the stove.

"Good morning."

He stood and came over to her, wrapped his arms around her waist and kissed her neck.

"Thank you for a wonderful night. There's no going back for us now. Are you all right with that?"

She turned in his arms, her gaze lifting to meet his. "I came out here to get married and help people, in that order and so far I seem to be doing both, so yes, I'm fine with our situation. What about you?" *The chain around her neck seemed heavier. Guilt for wearing it?*

He pulled her close and looked down at her. "I'm good with the decision. I never thought I'd like being married, but so far I do and I even like having a child."

"She's doing very well with all the changes." She smoothed the collar on his shirt. "This is all very new for her and she is, after all, only three."

"I know. I just see how she is with Walt and wish she could like me as much as she likes him."

A gasp sounded. Her eyes widened. "You're jealous…of Walt?"

"I'm not."

She laughed. "You are. Just remember, she spends all day every day with Walt. He's like her beloved grandfather. You're still an unknown quantity. Someone who has taken her mother from her."

A frown wrinkled his brow. "I didn't—"

"You did, but it's not your fault. It's mine. After Adam was murdered, I took to sleeping with Melly. So now that I'm sleeping with you, she sees it as me abandoning her."

"Well, she'd better get used to it because I'm not giving you back." He hugged her close and rested his chin on her head. "I like having you in my bed."

She looked down at the floor, heat gathering in her core as she remembered what they did in that bed.

"I like being in your bed...our bed." She laughed. "I've never enjoyed not sleeping with anyone more."

"I'm very gratified to hear that. I want you to take pleasure in the marriage bed. Having marital relations shouldn't be something done just because it's expected, but rather because it is enjoyed. By both parties."

"Mama."

Jeremiah groaned and released Alice.

"Melly." Alice reached up and patted her hair. "Are you hungry, sweetheart?"

The child nodded and then cocked her head. "Why'd Doc have his arms 'round you?"

"We were just saying good morning. Doc and I hug each other when we say good morning."

"Why?"

"Because we are married and we like each other." *Doesn't she remember her father and I doing this very thing? Is she forgetting him already?*

"I don't want to do that." Melly wrinkled her nose.

"You don't want to do what? Say good

morning? Or is it you don't want a hug?"

"Hug."

Alice squatted so she'd be eye level with her daughter. *Breakfast can wait. Melly needs me.* "You don't have to get a hug. It's all right if you don't."

"I want you to…not him."

Melly pointed at Jeremiah.

"That's all right for now, too. As you get to know Doc, you'll probably change your mind, but that is entirely up to you. Isn't that right, Jeremiah?"

He knelt on one knee so he too was eye level with the child.

"What your mother says is true, Melly. If you don't want me to hug you, I won't. But I hope you'll feel differently, because I want to be your friend more than anything."

The little girl didn't smile. All she said was, "Maybe."

"That's all I ask. Now how about we let your mama fix breakfast? Are you hungry?"

She nodded.

"Good. So am I. What are we having for breakfast, Mama?"

"We're all having scrambled eggs, bacon and fried toast. When Walt gets here we'll eat."

"Sounds good to me, how about you, Melly? Does that sound good to you?"

Her hold on Alice relaxed a bit and she nodded.

"Why don't you sit at the table with me and let Mama do the cooking? Okay?"

He stood and held out his hand.

Melly looked around at her mother and then back at Doc before taking his hand. They walked the few steps to the table together.

Alice gazed at her daughter's face and wondered if trouble was brewing.

# CHAPTER 7

June 15, 1873

Standing next to her husband in the surgery room, Alice watched Jeremiah wash the soap lather from his hands after treating the last patient, another child with chickenpox.

"I'm glad that you practice cleanliness. I believe many of the diseases we see are transmitted through filth and unclean ways."

"So do I. I'm always telling my patients to keep themselves clean, but most times the advice falls on deaf ears."

"Why haven't I seen any Chinese people come here for treatment? Do they have their own doctors?"

He finished drying his hands and set the towel on the counter in the surgery, next to the pitcher and basin. A washcloth and soap bar also sat on the counter.

"I don't know. They must have. I'm told disease seems to be rampant in the Chinese part of town. I get miners in here all the time who have caught something from the Chinese prostitutes."

She waved her hand. "How do you know the sicknesses are from the Chinese? Why couldn't the disease have come from somewhere else?"

"Didn't you know? All those diseases…like smallpox, syphilis, gonorrhea and leprosy…come from the Chinese."

She frowned and shook her head. "That's just not true and you know it."

He cocked his head. "Of course, I know that. Don't you recognize sarcasm when you hear it? But, what I also know is the white prostitutes that I treat don't have those diseases and the miners that come in do. They have to have gotten them somewhere and I only know what they tell me."

"If that's the case why haven't we seen a major smallpox outbreak?"

"Well, that was just an example. We haven't gotten anyone with smallpox…yet. So far it's just been syphilis and gonorrhea, but we will you just wait and see."

"That's ridiculous," said Alice

"Maybe. Most white people have been inoculated against smallpox and I've never seen a case of leprosy. Have you?"

She shook her head. "No, I haven't, at least not yet. We're liable to see anything here."

"What did you see in your practice?" asked Jeremiah.

"To be honest, I didn't treat many patients. Adam and I married soon after my graduation and then I was pregnant with Melly. Adam refused to have me work while I was pregnant. He didn't want me to get anything contagious."

He crossed his arms over his chest.

"So basically, you are arguing with me just to be argumentative."

"Well, I just think we should help those people if we can."

He shrugged.

"How do you propose we do that if they don't come to the office?"

"We could go to them. Set up an office in the Chinese portion of town."

He rolled his eyes.

"We have all the patients I can handle now."

She pointed at him. "All *you* can handle." Alice pressed her hand to her chest. "I'm a fully qualified doctor and I want to help people. Acting as your nurse is not enough."

Jeremiah closed his eyes and pinched the skin between them.

"I thought we'd been through this. You would act as my nurse until I thought you could handle—"

Alice put her hands on her hips. "I've been your nurse for more than a month and you aren't any more likely to want me to continue as anything but your nurse. I am a doctor and a good one, which you would know if you'd give me a chance. I've read every medical text you have and every medical paper published we've been able to get our hands on."

"Very well. You and I will work side-by-side today, only you'll be doing the diagnosing. If you have any new ideas or ways of doing things I'd like to see them. Your education is much more recent and keeping up with the new advances in medicine is very difficult."

She narrowed her eyes. "Really? Just like that you'll give me a chance? I don't have to plead or beg, just ask?"

"Just like that. You do realize that by taking on a whole new group of patients in the Chinese, I'll be right back to the same problem I had before you came—too many patients for one person."

She relaxed. "We'll work it out together. Shall we go to work?"

"We shall." He looked around. "Walt has already taken Melly for the day, I see."

"Yes, they're going on a picnic to Walt's cabin. I fixed them a lunch and he's promised me he won't let her play in the creek."

"Did they go on horseback? Has Melly ridden before?"

"They are. Walt will hold her in front of him and he promised he wouldn't gallop with her."

"He'll do what he says. He's a good man and loves that little girl more than anything."

Alice took a deep breath and sighed. "I didn't know what to expect when I came to Hope's Crossing, but finding a new grandfather for Melly, was definitely not one the things I contemplated. Melly's grandfather died just a few months before Adam. They were very close, just as she is with Walt."

Jeremiah chuckled. "Finding you and Melly isn't what Walt expected either. You have both been so good for each other."

She took the two steps to him and put her arms around his neck. "And you? What did you expect?"

"Not you. You're the most unexpected bride a man could have. A fully qualified doctor, who is beautiful besides. How could I have expected that?"

"You do say the nicest things." She brought his head down to hers and kissed him softly before letting him go again. "I'd better not do any more than that for now. Make you anxious for tonight."

He grinned. "I hunger for you every night."

She smiled, turned and walked toward the clinic. Then she turned back and winked, watched him flush and shake his head. She laughed as she walked on to their destination.

The day was long. The last two patients she had were a baby girl with jaundice and ten-year-old boy with a broken arm. Broken bones were one of the things she had a difficult time with.

"Doctor Kilarney, will you set the boy's arm while I get the plaster of Paris ready, please?"

"Certainly."

When the process was complete, the boy and his mother on their way, Jeremiah stood with his hands out in front of him, covered in white goop.

"Why didn't you set the arm yourself?"

"I don't have the strength to do it properly. I can set it if I must, but doing so can be difficult on the patient because I can't do it quickly, often having to try a couple of times." She poured water in the basin for him to wash his hands of the plaster. "I'm not ashamed of my limitations. I know them and as long as you are here, you can help me with them."

"I'm happy to hear that you recognize you're not as strong as me, as a man."

After he was done cleaning his hands, she stepped over to the pitcher of water and the basin beside it on the counter along the wall. There she thoroughly washed the plaster off her hands and emptied the basin into a bucket on the floor.

"Of course, I do. I'm well aware of the differences between men and women. I did very well in my anatomy classes."

"What did you specialize in?"

"I was a surgical resident at Pittsburgh's Women's Hospital."

"Surgery. That may be very useful. I'm not a surgeon, though I've had to force myself to be on a number of occasions."

"I would imagine so. After all you are the only doctor in the area."

"But now, if you can do the surgeries, I won't have to. How sharp are your skills."

"Sharper than yours are, I'm sure."

"*Touché.* Shall we?"

"Yes, doctor."

He swept his arm toward the door.

"After all, we don't want to keep our patients waiting."

\*\*\*\*\*

A week later, Alice was in the kitchen fixing dinner.

"Mama, I don't feel good."

She turned at the sound of her daughter's voice.

"Melly, come here baby. What's wrong?"

"I don't feel good."

She scratched her belly through her clothes.

"Oh dear. Let me see your tummy, sweetheart." *I knew this would happen when I put the play area in the clinic.*

Alice raised Melly's dress and saw what she expected. A red rash over her stomach.

"Okay. You stay right there. I'm getting Jeremiah."

She walked into the living room where Jeremiah sat reading the latest medical book.

"Jeremiah. Melly has chickenpox. I need you to finish dinner so I can bathe her and help her to feel better."

"Of course."

He set the book aside.

"Are you sure? You want me to look at her?"

Alice rolled her eyes and crossed her arms over her chest.

"I'm a fully-qualified doctor. Why would I need you to look at her?"

"Sorry. Old habits die hard. What will you do for her?"

"I'll give her an oatmeal bath and then put on her nightgown. If you'd heat a kettle of water, I'll make her some willow bark tea."

Smiling, he nodded.

"That's what I'd do, too. If you'll finish

dinner and put on the kettle, I'll fill a metal bucket with water, put it on the stove to heat and get the bathtub."

"Thank you. I appreciate the assistance."

"That's what married people do. Help each other."

"I'm sorry for snapping at you earlier. I know you were only trying to help."

He walked over and put his arms around her, offering nothing more than comfort.

"I'm not the best husband all the time, but I try. Melly means a lot to me and I don't want to see her uncomfortable or in pain."

"I know and I thank you for that." Alice leaned into the strength of his embrace. She's not been exactly warm toward you."

"She's scared of what she doesn't understand. When she sees that I'm not taking you away from her, she'll settle down."

Minutes later, Alice took the hot water bucket off the stove and poured half of it into the tub sitting in the middle of the kitchen floor, saving the other half to rinse Melly with, and then she added a full bucket of cold water to the tub. The bath was just lukewarm and that's what she wanted. She added a cup of oatmeal to the water and then helped her daughter into the tub. She used a wash cloth to put the soothing water over Melly's back and shoulders.

"Lie back sweetie, I want to rinse your hair, too. Doesn't your head itch?"

Melly whimpered and nodded.

"I itch all over."

Tears fell from her eyes and she cried softly.

That sound hurt Alice more than if she'd been screaming. The low whimpers from her daughter struck her deep in her heart.

"I know you do, sweetie. This will help. Stand so I can rinse you."

Melly stood shivering in the now cold water.

As quickly as she could, Alice poured the warm water from the bucket over her head. When she was done, she wrapped a towel around Melly and lifted her from the tub. She set her on the floor and patted her dry, not wanting to trigger the itching by rubbing her vigorously like she usually did. Then she wrapped the towel around her again and carried Melly to her bedroom to put on her nightgown and socks on both her hands and feet.

I want you to put the socks on your hands whenever you are not eating. Understand?"

She nodded. "Uh huh."

"Good. Are you hungry?"

Melly shrugged.

She worried about Melly's lack of energy and appetite. "You have to eat something, sweetie. Let's go see about dinner."

Alice had fried porkchops and was making gravy when Melly had made her announcement. Jeremiah finished the gravy and put on a pan of oatmeal.

"I wasn't sure she'd be able to eat regular. But she needs to keep up her strength and I thought oatmeal might sit better on her tummy."

Alice's heart melted a little. He was showing so much concern for her baby, how could she not find that attractive?

She hugged him. "Thank you, so much."

"Here now. No tears. You'll scare her."

Alice hadn't realized she'd been crying. She wiped her face with the hem of her apron and then turned to Melly.

"Come on, sweetheart. Let's get you seated and get some food in you. What do you want? Oatmeal? I'll make you some toast if you like."

"No toast." She wrinkled her nose as though she would cry.

"As you wish, Miss Melly," said Doc. He dished up a small amount and handed it to Alice. "I don't know how she likes her oatmeal fixed."

"It's all right. I'll get it. You want milk and sugar, don't you sweetie?"

Alice poured milk and sprinkled sugar into the bowl, and then stirred it all together until it was smooth.

"Here you go, sweetie."

She put the bowl down in front of Melly.

The child looked at the food and started to cry.

"What's the matter, sweetheart?"

"I don't want oatmeal."

"That's fine, calm down what do you want?"

Melly sniffled. "Fried toast."

Alice closed her eyes. *First she doesn't want toast and now she does. She really doesn't feel good.* "All right I'll make you fried toast. Why don't you eat a little of the oatmeal until the toast is ready?"

"Okay," she whimpered.

Doc crouched next to Melly's chair.

"Melly, sweetheart, will you let me look in your mouth please?"

"Why?"

"Tell me something. Does your throat hurt or your mouth when you swallow?"

She nodded and opened her mouth.

"Say ahhh for me," said Doc.

"Ahhhh," said Melly.

"Jeremiah? Does she have sores in her mouth?"

"Just a couple, but enough to make eating uncomfortable. She'd be better off with soup, broth would be even better."

"Oh, honey. Why didn't you tell me your mouth hurt?"

Melly shrugged and tears ran down her cheeks.

"Come here." Alice picked up her daughter and then sat in the chair with her.

"Jeremiah, look for the leftover chicken soup from lunch in the icebox. Will you heat it, please? I think I'll just hold my sweet girl for a while."

"Sure thing. You two sit at the table. The soup will be ready in no time."

Heating the soup didn't take long and when it was warm, not hot, he dished up a bowl for his step-daughter.

"Here you go. Let's see if this doesn't make our girl feel better."

"I not you girl," insisted Melly.

"Whatever you say, sweetheart," said Alice. "But for now you need to eat this soup. Then I'll put some cream on your rash and you can go to sleep."

She spooned a bit of soup into Melly's mouth.

When her daughter finished the entire bowl, Alice set the spoon in the dish.

"You did very well, eating all the soup that Doc prepared. Can you thank him?"

Melly shook her head.

"It's all right," said Jeremiah. "She doesn't feel good. We'll have lots more chances to get her to accept me, because I'm not going anywhere."

"Thank you, for understanding. I'm surprised she says good night to you, but I won't look a gift horse in the mouth."

"I think she hopes if she says goodnight, that I won't be there in the morning."

Alice laughed. "You may be right."

"Then she'll be greatly disappointed because I intend to be here every morning."

"I'm glad to hear it."

Alice carried Melly to her bedroom and got the rose cream. She put it everywhere her daughter had spots.

"Does that feel a little better?"

Melly nodded and then whimpered again.

Alice wanted to cry herself. She hated it when Melly was sick for any reason. This time she knew she could get worse and wondered what the morning would bring.

# CHAPTER 8

Dick Lane watched the building where the doctor and his whore practiced medicine. He couldn't think of Alice Carter as anything but a whore. Her husband hadn't been dead but six months and she was already married again. The world would be better off with one less woman of ill repute.

His own circumstance didn't matter. Living with a prostitute was a necessary evil. He was doing what he needed to in order to be close to Alice. *But Rebecca has only been gone for nine months, am I any better? No I won't think about that. I'm not that person. That person died with Rebecca.*

But what about the little girl? His conscience kept popping up and reminding him that he'd be leaving the child an orphan. He thought about his own daughter, Jane. She was being raised by her grandmother now. He knew he wasn't a fit father. Not without his Rebecca. Jane was better off with her grandmother, than with him.

He thought the old woman would understand his need for vengeance. After all, it was her daughter who was murdered. But even she had looked askance when he told her his intentions.

"Dick, don't do this. I understand how you feel, truly I do. No one, even you, miss her more than I do. But you have a little girl of your own who needs you, her father, not me. I raised my daughter, now it's time you stepped up to raise yours."

"I can't. Not yet. I have to kill her. Alice Carter. She was there. She assisted, so she is as culpable as her husband was."

"Dick. Please."

"I can't, Ruth. It has to be this way. Take care of Jane for me."

Ruth shook her head. "You're going to get yourself killed. Where will Jane be then?"

"She'll be with you and better off than if she was with me."

He'd left then. Didn't even hug Jane goodbye because he couldn't bear to see her cry.

*****

Alice walked through the encampment of the Chinese miners. They were very hard workers, but kept to themselves pretty much. They had their own town, with a mercantile and butcher. They relied on themselves and the animals they raised for food and seemed to have no use for the white man.

Even so, Alice looked for a storefront to open a clinic to treat them. She was sure if a doctor was available, they would come.

At every empty space she found, the owner said "Rented. You no rent."

Finally, one of the Chinese men approached her.

"Lady doctor, no one here will rent to you. We have own doctor. Man. Chinese. Go back where you come from."

*Well, I guess they really don't want help. At least I tried.*

Defeated, she walked back to the office.

Jeremiah came out to the waiting area.

"Where have you been? Come with me to the surgery, please.".

Alice followed him. "I went to the Chinese encampment. I looked for a potential location for the clinic."

When they reached the surgery,

Jeremiah closed the door after them and leaned against it.

"And how did that go?

"Not well, if you must know. And I'd appreciate you not saying 'I told you so.'"

"You knew I didn't want you to go, and you went anyway. Why?"

She put her hands on her hips. "Because I want to help. I want to be a doctor."

"We've been seeing patients together and I've seen how well you do—"

"But not enough to let me see patients alone."

"If you'll let me finish. I intended to let you see patients on your own today and see how it goes, but I'm not sure you have the correct attitude."

She smiled and ran to him. "Oh, Jeremiah. Really? You're not funning me?"

"I'm not funning you. And as to the Chinese, actually, I'm sorry you were unsuccessful. I would love to have a way of helping those people as well, but I never had the time or the energy to do what you did."

She smiled and kissed him.

He put his arms around her and kissed her back.

She would have been perfectly happy to

have stayed in his arms and kissed him all morning long, but real life intruded, as always, when a patient arrived, badly injured and carried on a stretcher.

All three of the men were filthy, covered in loose dirt and sweat. She couldn't even tell what color their hair was through the coating of soil.

The man on the stretcher was just as dirty. She saw where they bandaged him around the chest and stomach, but the bandages were soaked through. He was still bleeding profusely and if the blood was as dark as it appeared, more than likely he was bleeding inside as well.

"This way gentlemen." Seeing no need to stop in the examination room, she led the two men carrying the man on the stretcher straight to the surgery.

"What happened?" asked Jeremiah.

"Cave-in. Andy here got caught in it. We had to dig him out," said one of the miners. "Do you think you can help him?"

"I don't know, but we'll do the best we can," said Jeremiah as he cut away the injured mans clothes.

"Why don't you men wait in the other room while Doc does his work?"

"Yes, ma'am," said the taller of the two men. "But actually, we got to get back to work. Jesse will be down to wait for Andy."

"This happened at Jesse Donovan's mine?" asked Jeremiah.

"Just about two hours ago. It took us that long to dig him out. Jesse went to see to Andy's family. He's got two kids, boy and a girl, nine and ten. After that he'll come here."

The men turned and left.

Jeremiah had removed the man's clothes and was checking him for internal injuries by pressing on his stomach. They saw the deep gash just to the side on his torso, from which the blood was flowing but that's not what worried her or Jeremiah.

"He's hemorrhaging inside, likely ruptured his spleen."

He looked up at her.

"Can you operate on him?"

Alice swallowed hard. This was the chance she'd been waiting for but could she do it? What if she lost him, like she and Adam had lost Rebecca? Could she face that outcome?

"I can, but I won't guarantee I can save him. His recovery will depend on the injuries I find inside."

She walked to the counter, poured water into the basin from the pitcher next to it and cleaned her hands thoroughly using lye soap.

"Do you have ether to give him? He's passed out now, but when I start cutting, he may wake and you should be prepared."

"I have ether and I'll be ready to assist in any way I can. Are you ready to proceed?"

She nodded and walked over to the injured man using a rag dipped in boric acid, Alice cleaned him as much as possible around the site of her incision, from his breast bone to his pelvis. Then she opened him up and looked at each of his organs for injuries. There were small tears on his liver, but they weren't what was causing all the bleeding. His spleen had indeed ruptured. She sutured the injured site closed with stitches as small as she could make them. The bleeding stopped. She used clean rags to remove the blood out of the area and looked for any other injuries but didn't see any.

"All right, I'll close now."

She sutured several layers of the incision closed, again using very small stitches.

"Now let's check the rest of him."

She and Jeremiah checked Andy over carefully. He had many abrasions and places that were starting to bruise on his arms and head. Several cuts on his face needed closing, as well as a long gash on his leg. Together she and Jeremiah managed to get him sewn up.

Once they were done, both went to the basin. Alice poured the used water into the bucket on the floor. She emptied half the pitcher into the basin and scrubbed her hands with the lye soap. Jeremiah did the same. She poured the rest of the water over their hands to rinse away the soap.

"Where are we putting Andy after he awakes? We don't have facilities for inpatient care."

"I'll talk to Jesse when he arrives, if he is not here already. Let's go see."

In the waiting room sat a tall, dark-haired man and two children, both with light brown hair and dark eyes.

Jeremiah came forward into the waiting room and took Jesse's hand.

"Jesse. I'm glad you're here. Are these Andy's children?"

Jesse put his hands on the children's

shoulders.

"Yes. This is Mary and John Reed, Andy's kids. How is their father?"

"Yes, please how is Daddy?"

Mary crushed her skirt in her hands.

Jeremiah pulled over a chair and sat at the girl's level. His voice was calm, his words measured.

"I think your papa will recover fine."

"When will he be able to go back to work?" asked Jesse.

Alice saw red. Her eyes widened and then narrowed. "Mr. Donovan. This man has been grievously injured in your mine. Please allow him the time to heal before you put him back to work."

"I'm sorry Alice. I was trying to determine how long he'll need help. I intend to have someone care for him."

"I'll look after Daddy." Mary's hands were now fists at her sides.

"Mary," said Alice gently. "Your father will need care that you might not be able to give him."

"Then I'll help," said John, as fiercely as his sister.

Alice took a breath and opened her mouth to speak.

Jeremiah put a hand on her arm and stopped her.

"You two can take care of him. Mary can you cook?"

The little girl was only ten, but she had a strength about her that surprised Alice.

"I'm a good cook. My ma taught me before she passed."

"That's good," said Jeremiah. "But I'll send over some broth and dinner for you two from the restaurant for this first night. You'll have to keep a good eye on him and I don't want you to worry about supper. I'll come and check on him tomorrow."

"Thank you."

The girl's brown eyes were full of angry tears.

"And I'll see that you have plenty of food. I'll deliver your meals myself everyday when I come to check on your father."

Alice could almost hear what would happen next before it did.

Mary turned on Jesse.

"Why did he get hurt?

Jesse knelt in front of her. "I don't know Mary, but I'll get to the bottom of this and find out why. I promise."

Her shoulders sagged and she sniffled, looked at him and nodded.

He waited and then opened his arms. Mary and John both went to Jesse and let him hold them for a few moments.

Mary was the first to break away. She wiped her eyes with the back of her hand and sniffled.

"Will you be able to carry him home for us?" she asked Jesse.

"Yes," he answered. "If Doc here can come with me we will get him into the house. Doc?"

Jeremiah gazed at Alice. "Will you be all right here while I'm gone? What about Melly?"

Alice nodded. "Walt is taking care of Melly and I'll be fine here. Go and help Jesse."

He walked over to her and kissed her cheek.

"You are amazing. If the children weren't present, I'd kiss you the way you deserve," he whispered in her ear and then kissed it.

She smiled, couldn't help it.

Jesse and Jeremiah lifted Andy onto the stretcher on the floor and Jeremiah set his doctor's bag in-between Andy's feet before picking up the stretcher.

Mary went before them opening the doors and John followed.

Alice followed them out and was surprised to find several people in the waiting room, all watching the men carry out Andy. A couple of miners got up and helped take Andy out to the wagon. They didn't return and she assumed they were escorting the injured man all the way home.

"All right ladies and gentlemen, I'll see you in Doc's stead. If there is something that I don't know, we'll wait for Doc to return, but I'm assuming you'd like to be treated as soon as possible."

The people looked around at each other. Finally a young man came forward.

"What can I do for you, Mister...?" asked Alice.

"Danvers. Melvin Danvers."

"Hello, Mr. Danvers. What can I do for you?"

"I just got to town and my wife, June, is sickly."

"Where is your wife?"

"She can't come in."

Alice took out a sheet of paper. "Tell me

her symptoms. How is she feeling? Is she coughing? Does she have a fever?"

"Yes, ma'am. Both those things and she's got a rash, too."

*Oh, dear Lord. What if she has smallpox?*

"Were you both inoculated against smallpox?"

"Yes, ma'am we were."

*Thank God*

"It sounds like she has the chicken pox but I won't know until I see her. For now give her willow bark tea, and if she itches, give her a bath in warm water with a cup of oatmeal added."

"Yes, ma'am. Thank you. What do I owe you?"

"You're welcome. For a consultation such as that, just a quarter. Write directions to your home on a sheet of paper on the desk."

"Yes, ma'am." He handed her the quarter she asked for. "All right who's next?"

She saw the patients as quickly as she could and still give each one the time they needed to explain their problems.

When Jeremiah returned only two

people sat in the waiting room.

"Where did everyone go?"

"I treated them, and they went home or back to their jobs."

Both of his eyebrows rose.

"You treated them?"

"Are you surprised? That they let me treat them was a surprise to me. I think having been your nurse for the last month has given them faith in my abilities. I guess they figure if you can trust me, so can they."

He came forward and hugged her.

"I'm very proud of you. Let's go back to the surgery."

"Thank you." She turned to the patients waiting. "I'll be with you in a few minutes."

Once they reached the surgery, Alice sat in the single chair. Jeremiah leaned against the counter.

"Did you get Andy settled? Did he wake up?"

"The answer to both of those questions is yes. He was in quite a lot of pain."

"Understandable."

"I gave Mary a bottle of laudanum with the instructions to put a dropper full in half a glass of water and give it to him every four hours. That should help keep him comfortable."

"Good. I hope Mary and John are up to the task of caring for their father. He'll be too sore at first to do anything but sleep mostly but as he gets better and wants to get up and around, I'm afraid he'll get surly with them." *I'll write down the instructions for Mary. She's got a lot to do and the details of the medicine can be hard for a ten-year-old to remember.*

"I'll talk to them and to him. Hopefully we can avoid that situation."

"Thank you."

"I'm the one who should be thanking you. That man is alive because of your skills…not mine."

"Thank you. I'm proud that my *skills* were still up to the task. It's been four years since I did surgery. How long do you think he'll be down?" Hearing him acknowledge her skills felt incredibly satisfying.

"Not as long as we want him to be. I want him home for six weeks, but I'll take out the stitches in about ten days and he'll want to go back to work then. They always do, even though Jesse tells them he'll take care of them."

"Why don't you wait and take out the

stitches after three weeks? As to him going back to work, I understand. He's proud and doesn't want to take what he sees as a handout. Money he hasn't earned. And maybe what Jesse should tell him is that this is just an advance of his wages and that he'll have to pay him back. Maybe then Andy would stay down the time they needed." She sighed. "I don't know."

"I'll suggest it to Jesse, but I'm afraid then Andy would be even more likely to get back to work too soon. He wouldn't want to owe Jesse any more than he has to." Jeremiah shook his head. "I wish I knew the answer."

"We need to see those last two patients then we can close the office. It's past six."

"You're right. They've waited long enough."

Back in the waiting room were a woman who was clearly pregnant and a man with a bandage on his arm.

Jeremiah took the man and the woman went with Alice.

"What can I do for you Mrs. Grayson?"

"Doc wanted me to come in so he could check and see if our original due date was correct. I think he just wanted to check this pregnancy and assure me and him that all was well. I've lost two children before and he been keeping a close eye on me."

"Let's get you up on the table and take a peek."

Mrs. Grayson used the small step stool and climbed onto the table.

Alice examined her.

"You look to be about seven-and-one-half to eight months pregnant. Basically, you could have this baby in about a month. Is that what you and Dr. Kilarney came up with?"

Alice helped the woman to sit up.

Mrs. Grayson beamed.

"Yes, I should be eight months now according to Doc's calculations."

Alice smiled.

"Good. I bet you're ready to have this baby. I was when I was expecting my daughter. When I reached eight months I couldn't wait to have her. I was so tired of being pregnant."

"Oh, I don't mind. After losing two babies, as long as this one is healthy I don't mind carrying him at all."

"Good. That's good. Here let me help you down."

Alice held Mrs. Grayson's hand and she slid off the table.

"Thank you, Mrs. Kilarney. I appreciate the help. Oh,"

Her eyebrows raised, Mrs. Grayson looked at the floor. Liquid spread from under her skirt.

"Well. Looks like you're having this baby today. I want you to start walking around the room. I find the movement helps the labor go more quickly. I'll get Jeremiah."

# CHAPTER 9

Alice ran down the hall to the surgery where Jeremiah was treating the man with the cut on his arm. Jeremiah put the finishing touches on his bandage.

"I want you to keep this wound clean and dry. If you need to, change the bandage every day."

"Sure thing, Doc. Hello, Mrs. Kilarney."

"Hello…"

"Timothy. Timothy Nubbins."

"Hello, Timothy. If you'll excuse us, I need to talk to Doc."

"You're free to go Tim," said Jeremiah.

"Thanks, Doc."

Jeremiah turned to Alice.

"What's wrong?"

"It's Mrs. Grayson. I just examined her to see how her pregnancy was proceeding and everything looked fine. As soon as she got up off the table, her water broke. That shouldn't have happened. There was no indication that she was that far along. She should have another month to go?"

"Let's go see what's happening. How many babies have you delivered?"

"None. I was a surgeon and I never had reason to consult on any pregnancies, so this would be my first."

"I'm sure Mrs. Grayson is fine. We've probably just made a mistake in her due date or perhaps the little one is coming a tad early. Don't panic. Everything will be okay."

"All right. I'm fine now."

They walked back to the examination room where Mrs. Grayson was. She was still walking in circles around the table in the center of the room.

"Hello, Doc. Did she tell you? I'm having this baby a little early."

"She told me Emma. How are you feeling?"

"Just Dandy. I haven't had any labor pains yet."

"Good. I need you to get back up on the table so I can check you."

She nodded and did as he asked.

"Raise your knees and open wide. I need

to see what the baby is doing."

"Okay."

Jeremiah checked and measured.

"The baby is not crowning or anything yet. I think we have time."

He listened to her stomach trying to find the baby's heartbeat. Finally he found it and smiled. Then he frowned just as quickly.

Jeremiah turned to Alice and mouthed, "I think he's breech."

Alice tried to keep her face expressionless so Emma wouldn't get worried.

He turned back to Emma. "We have to wait to see more when the baby starts to come."

Alice noticed Emma frowning and turning pale.

"Are you having a labor pain? You need to tell me when you do, so we can time them and know when the baby is arriving."

"Yes, pain."

Emma held her breath and shut her eyes.

"Emma. Breathe. Not breathing doesn't help. You need to breathe regular."

"All right."

For the next six hours they watched and waited.

"The baby is trying to come fast. I measured her at a nine."

Jeremiah nodded.

"Did you see the head?"

"No. I think you'll have to turn it or we'll have to do a caesarian section."

"I'll try to turn him."

"Emma, the baby is turned around and not coming the right way. I'll try to turn him. It will be painful and I just want you prepared."

"Do what you have to, just make sure my baby is all right."

"We're doing everything we can."

Jeremiah reached in.

"I feel a leg in the birth canal. I'm pushing it back up and turning the baby."

He pushed and pulled and got the baby turned.

"All right he's facing the right way and is in the proper position."

Two hours later Jeremiah, pulled a baby boy from his mother.

"Alice, clean up this fine boy for his mother."

"Yes, doctor."

She walked to the counter and cleaned the baby and weighed him. She wrapped him in a little blanket that the baby's father had brought and gave the infant to his mother.

Emma, tears pouring down her face, held her arms up to receive her baby.

Alice laid the crying baby in his mother's arms. "You did just fine Emma. Just fine. He's a little small, only six pounds, but looks to be healthy and as you can hear, he has a fine set of lungs."

*****

Sunday, August 17, 1873

Two weeks after the incident with Andy Reed, they were sitting at the kitchen table after they had gone to church with Walt and Melly. Melly was now healthy again and was now reading in the living room with Walt.

"Jeremiah."

"Yes?" he said absentmindedly while reading the paper.

"Look at me, please."

He lowered the paper, his brows furrowed.

"Why haven't you told anyone that I did the surgery on Andy?"

He took a deep breath. "The situation is

very complicated. I didn't want to tell everyone and have Andy die, so I've been waiting for him to recover enough to return to work. I didn't want anyone to blame you if he died."

She cocked her head and lowered her chin. "That's very kind of you. I was afraid it was because you still didn't believe I am a real doctor."

"After what I saw you do in the operating room and seeing how well Andy has recovered...how could I be anything but a believer? You proved yourself to me over and over and I've been lax in letting the town know about your abilities. I'll fix that. I'll post a story in the newspaper and put your name on the sign out front. It will read, Dr. Jeremiah Kilarney and Dr. Alice Carter Kilarney. What do you think?"

Alice smiled wide, went to Jeremiah and sat in his lap.

"I think that's wonderful. Thank you. When will you put the story in the paper?"

"I'll take it down to Effie today. It will run in tomorrow's paper."

"What will it say?"

He took a folded piece of paper from his shirt pocket.

"I've already written it. Tell me what you think."

*From the desk of Dr. Jeremiah Kilarney:*

*I would like to welcome to Hope's Crossing and to my practice, Dr. Alice Carter Kilarney. Dr. Kilarney is a surgeon and a much-needed addition to our town. She has already proved her skill in the surgical treatment of Andy Reed after he was severely injured in a cave-in at the Donovan mine.*

*With Dr. Kilarney now working in this office, not only will we be able to see more patients in a shorter period of time but now we have a skilled surgeon in our town. Hopefully between the two of us we will meet the needs of our community in a more complete manner.*

*If you have any questions either I or Dr. Alice would be happy to alleviate your concerns so don't hesitate to call on us.*

When she finished, she let the paper float to the table, took her husband's head in her palms and kissed him.

She pulled back and rested her hands on his shoulders. "Thank you. That is a wonderful letter to the community. I hope people read it and realize they shouldn't be afraid of having me treat them as a doctor, not just as your nurse."

"I wouldn't expect a change in their attitudes overnight, but it is a start"

*****

Monday morning, Dick Lane watched and waited, hidden in the shadows of the alley across from the clinic. He was patient biding his time, waiting to get her alone. But time was running out for him. His money was running out. If he didn't take care of her soon, he'd have to go to work in the mines to survive.

Getting her alone might be easier now. He watched the doctor put a new sign up on the white picket fence that surrounded the doctor's home and office.

*Dr. Jeremiah Kilarney*
*Dr. Alice Kilarney*

So he was recognizing her as a doctor. But she wasn't a doctor. She was a murderer and she'd get hers soon enough. Now though the doctor would let her be alone in the office or make house calls. That would be the best, catch her on her way to or from someone's house.

He nodded, though no one was there to see.

Yes, that would be the best. But he needed a place to take her. He wanted her to admit she'd killed Rebecca.

He'd discovered when he killed her husband that he'd gained no satisfaction in just killing him. He needed her to *admit* her mistake, *admit* she was wrong. *Admit* she'd murdered Rebecca. That was the only way he could have peace.

He walked away, back to the Branch Water Saloon. Tomorrow or the next day he'd have his opportunity. He had to be prepared to pounce when the time came.

*****

Monday night, Alice was in the kitchen and had just given Melly a bath. She wasn't one of those people who only bathed once a week. She bathed Melly and herself every other day. She believed that cleanliness helped prevent illnesses. Luckily, Jeremiah was of the same mind.

Now she was getting Melly ready for bed. Alice was gratified that Melly was learning to accept Jeremiah. She let him read to her at night without Alice being present and she'd begun to take his hand when the three of them walked to the mercantile together.

She pulled Melly's nightgown over her head.

"Mama."

"Yes, Melly, what do you need?"

"Would Doc mind if I called him Daddy?"

Alice put Melly's robe on her, followed by her slippers.

"I'm sure he wouldn't mind but would be very pleased. Do you want to call him Daddy?"

"Not sure. Still thinkin'."

"Well, when you've made up your mind just let me know."

"'kay."

She skipped off to her bedroom.

Alice shook her head and smiled after her daughter. Oh, that Alice could have that kind of energy after a long day.

*****

Tuesday, August 19, 1873

"Where is Walt? He knows I don't hold meals, especially breakfast." She frowned concerned.

"Maybe he slept late," said Jeremiah. "I wouldn't worry about it."

"You might not, but I do. He wouldn't

let Melly be alone without letting us know beforehand."

"Well," Jeremiah put down his paper, went to the window. "Now that you mention it, he has been very regular about watching her every day."

"That's why I'm sure something has happened. I'll go see him as soon as we finish breakfast."

"No, I'll go. You tend to the patients that we have today."

"Well, it will be a good way to see if they will accept me, when it's not a matter of getting home for supper."

He nodded. "Think of being on your own for a while as a trial to see if the patients stay, knowing you're the doctor they'll see."

"What if they don't?"

He shrugged. "Well, then we'll have a lot more time on our hands. Might even get something else done for a change."

She cocked her head to the side. "Don't quip about this. I'm serious. What if the patients won't let me treat them?"

"We can't force them to be treated. If they won't let you, then they won't be treated. I'm taking the buggy and checking on Walt. If he's bad off, I'll bring him back here."

"If he's hurt, you might need help with him?"

"I'll see if I can get Sheriff Longworth to go with me."

Alice nodded.

"Be careful. Be safe."

"I will. You, too."

Jeremiah kissed her and walked out the door.

Alice smoothed her skirts and walked to Melly's room.

"Melly, you'll have to play by yourself today. Grandpa Walt hasn't come in yet. Doc went up to check on him. Okay?"

Melly nodded.

"Is Grandpa Walt okay?"

"I'm sure he is, but Doc will make sure."

Alice took Melly's hand in hers and patted it.

"Let's go sweetie."

*How will I handle patients and keep an eye on Melly, too?*

*****

"Sam!" Jeremiah went to the back of the jail and checked but no Sam.

Sam and Jo lived next door. He walked

over and knocked on the door.

Sam opened the front door.

"Hi Doc. What you doing here this time of morning?"

"I'm headed up to Walt Rogers's cabin. He didn't show up for breakfast and Alice is sure something is wrong. I can't say I disagree. I'd like you to come, too, if you would."

"Sure Doc. I've got to saddle my horse. You go on and I'll meet you there."

"Fine. See you in a few minutes."

Doc pulled up in front of Walt's cabin and set the brake before jumping down. He took his bag out of the back and walked up the path to pound on the door.

"Walt! Walt Rogers! Open up, it's Doc Kilarney."

Doc tried the door and found it open.

Sam rode up just as Doc was ready to go inside.

Sam drew his revolver.

"Let's go in together."

They went inside. The cabin was just one room with a kitchen area to the left, dining and living area in front of them and a sleeping area to the right.

Doc walked to the bed where Walt lay

uncovered, in his long red underwear, suspenders and pants.

"Walt."

Doc shook his shoulder. That's when he saw the darkened spot on his clothes.

"Geez, Walt. What did you do?"

"Doc?"

His voice was wheezy and just barely a whisper.

"Yes, it's me. I'm looking at that wound. Just stay where you are."

Doc opened the buttons on Walt's underwear down to his stomach, to expose the injury.

"I need you to sit up, Walt. I want to get this underwear off your arm so I can see the whole of your back." Doc lifted Walt's legs and turned them until they hung over the bedside, before he and Sam pulled the man into a sitting position.

Doc removed the underwear from both arms and peeled it down to Walt's waist. The wound was a hole about the size of a quarter. The skin around it was red and puffy. He bled profusely from the injury.

"I need to get you back to the office. Can you walk to the buggy if Sam and I help you?"

"I think so. My legs ain't hurt, I'm just weak."

"I won't worry about your clothes. I'll come back later for them."

"Take 'em now."

Walt had difficulty talking and wheezed out the words.

"Only. Two shirts. Coat on pegs by door.

"All right, stop trying to talk. I'll grab them when I get my case."

Sam and Jeremiah pulled Walt to his feet, and together they walked outside to the buggy. Walt's weight on Doc was slight. He seemed to be leaning against Sam more. Not that his weight would have been much anyway, Walt was even skinnier than Doc had been before Alice came.

They got him in the buggy, and Doc went back for Walt's clothes and the medical case he'd carried inside.

"You'll be staying with us. Do you know who shot you?"

"No."

"We'll take care of you. Alice will remove that bullet in no time."

Sam walked up carrying his horse's reins.

"Doc, can you get him back to town on your own. I'm staying to check the woods for leads. Maybe I can see where this would-be murderer got off to."

"Thanks Sam. I'd appreciate knowing that this person isn't out there waiting to finish the job. Walt has Melly with him most of the time." He looked over at Walt. "Guess it was lucky I came to check on you."

Walt was breathing a little easier sitting up, and better able to talk. "Nah, I knew you or Alice would come when I didn't show up today."

"You're lucky Melly loves you so much."

"She's got me wrapped around her little finger…and I like it."

Doc laughed. "I'm glad to see you still have your wits about you and your sense of humor, too." Twenty minutes later, they arrived back at Doc's offices.

Alice saw them and ran out to help. Together they got Walt inside and onto the table in the surgery.

"Granpa Walt," called Melly when they passed through the waiting room.

"Don't let her see me."

"Do you have him, Jeremiah?"

"Yes. See to Melly."

Alice took Walt's arm from around her neck and turned to catch Melly who was running up.

"Melly, sweetheart, Granpa Walt is hurt. Mama needs to take care of him. I want you to stay right here in this room. You color or play with your dolly or play jacks, but stay here. When Walt is better you can come see him, but Mama has to go now."

Tears ran down Melly's sweet face and the sight broke Alice's heart.

"You fix Granpa Walt?"

"Yes. I'll fix him. Now I have to go, sweetheart. I'll be back as soon as I can."

Alice hurried back to the surgery.

"Let me wash up and then I'll get you sewed up. Who shot you?"

"Don't know. Got me while I was doing chores and I don't think they were aiming for my shoulder."

"I have to make sure no bullet fragments remain in the wound. I don't want to stitch you up with anything left in there. Jeremiah, please hold him down. This will hurt."

He pinned Walt's shoulders to the table.

With clean hands Alice made a one inch incision on either side of the bullet hole, giving her fingers enough room to move without tearing the skin. She prodded the wound and found one good-sized fragment lodged against the bone.

Walt groaned and tried to get away from her questing fingers.

"You're lucky. I only feel one piece up against your shoulder bone. You won't be using that arm for a bit, while you heal."

"I don't feel lucky," said Walt.

She picked up the tweezers, put them in the wound and grabbed the bullet fragment, dropping it in an empty basin.

The metal slug piece hit with a resounding 'clunk'.

"I'll be pouring some alcohol into the wound to help kill any infection and it will hurt like the devil, but it has got to be done. Then I'll sew you up. You ready?"

"As ready as I'll ever be."

Alice took the bottle of alcohol and dribbled a stream into the wound.

Walt hollered and then fell silent.

She looked up at him and his eyes were closed. He'd passed out.

Alice smiled. "That makes things a lot easier."

She grabbed her needle and sutured the

wound closed.

"He can't be allowed to go back to his cabin alone." She walked to the basin and scrubbed her hands clean of the blood.

Jeremiah sighed. "Melly will have to sleep with us and Walt will sleep in her bed until he's healed."

"We need to do two things; expand the clinic to allow two rooms for in-patients and expand our house. We need a guest room and another bedroom for the nursery."

"Nursery?"

She grinned. "Now is probably not the best time to tell you, but I want you to understand that we really do need more room in the house. I wanted to wait until I was sure, but I am officially two months late. I'm having a baby. *We're* having a baby."

Jeremiah took her in his arms and swung her around in a circle.

"Yahoo!"

He put her down and kissed her tenderly, holding her face with his hands.

"Are you all right?"

She grinned, thrilled that he was so happy. "I'm terrific. I fully expect to work up until you deliver the baby."

"We'll see. I don't want you exerting yourself unnecessarily."

"I promise I won't do anything to hurt this baby. I want him…or her…as much as you do."

"I've got an idea to present to Jesse Donovan before I tell you."

"All right."

That afternoon, Doc went to the north end of town to see Jesse Donovan.

He knocked.

A pretty woman with beautiful fiery red hair answered the door.

"Doc. How nice to see you. Come in. Come in, please."

She stood to the side and let him pass.

"Hi Clare. I came to talk to Jesse. Is he here?"

"He is in his study. I'll take you there."

They entered a room that was more library than study. Bookshelves were floor to ceiling along the wall where they entered and the one to the left of the door. Directly across the room was a wall of windows. To the right was a fireplace in front of which was a sitting area with a sofa and two overstuffed chairs, all three upholstered in a rich blue brocade. Tall tables stood between the couch and the chairs and a low table in front of the sofa.

Sitting at a desk on the left side of the room, Jesse studied what looked like a ledger. Beneath the mahogany desk lay a burgundy Oriental rug with a paisley design in silver and gold.

Jesse looked up.

"Doc. What can I do for you?"

Doc took off his hat and rolled the brim in his hands before he sat in the leather chair in front of Jesse's desk. He leaned forward. "I'll come right to the point. I need a bigger house and clinic. We need two rooms where we can keep patients overnight. The house needs two more bedrooms since Alice is expecting and Walt Rogers is likely to be living with us for the time being."

Jesse stood, came around the desk and clapped Doc on the back.

Leaning back against the desk, Jesse crossed his arms over his chest. "Congratulations, Doc. I'd say you could now join the rest of us with sleepless nights but you do that now, with house calls at all hours. Why did you come to me with this request?"

Jeremiah rolled the brim of his hat in his

sweaty palms. "I want the mine owners to pay for the additions. They are the ones who benefit most since their workers will get better care. What do you say?"

Jesse was quiet a moment and moved back to his chair behind the desk.

"I'd say you're right, Doc. I'll bring it up at the meeting tomorrow night. You should have an answer the next morning. But I'm suggesting that our employees receive a discount on their visits. Seventy-five cents instead of one dollar. What do you think of that?"

"I agree."

"Then I'm sure your answer will be a positive one. Construction can start right away."

"Good. I'd like it finished before winter."

"I don't think that will be a problem. We can get people over there and get it up within the month."

Doc stood. "Thanks, Jesse."

"You're welcome, Doc. Let me know if you need anything else."

"I'll do it. I'll see myself out."

Doc went back to the clinic to find a couple of people waiting, Sam Longworth among them.

"Did you find anything?"

"Can we talk somewhere private?" Sam asked looking at the men sitting in the room, waiting to be seen by Doc or Alice.

"Sure. Follow me." He took Sam to the kitchen, poured them both a cup of lukewarm coffee and got the covered plate of molasses cookies off the top of the icebox.

After he placed the food and drink on the table he sat down.

"Tell me what you found."

"I found where the shooter waited for Walt. And I found his spent round. He only shot once. He either thought Walt was dead, or he wanted him wounded so you or Alice would come. My guess is he stood there and watched Walt stagger into the house." Sam rubbed his hand behind his neck. "He was waiting for one of you to show up. Since he didn't shoot you, I can only conclude that he was waiting for Alice."

"Alice!" Jeremiah jumped to his feet. "Why would anyone want to kill Alice?"

"I don't know. But I'd like to talk to her, if you don't mind."

"Sure, as long as I'm there when you

do." *Her husband was murdered, could the killer have followed her here?*

"Certainly. Why don't you three come down to dinner tonight? Melly can watch baby Paul, she's fascinated by him, and the rest of us can talk about who is stalking Alice."

## CHAPTER 10

Alice heated a cup of chicken broth for Walt before they went six blocks to the Longworth's house for dinner.

Jeremiah pulled the buggy out of the barn behind the house and made them take it, even though the evening was lovely.

Alice thought that was a bit strange, but decided he wanted to be prepared in case he had to leave on a house call. This was the first time they'd visited anyone in town. She made sure to wear her lavender dress to highlight her eyes. She dressed Melly in a lavender dress as well. It was made of the same material as her dress since she'd had them both made at the same time.

When they pulled up in front of the house, Jeremiah set the brake. Then he came around and first helped Alice down, before lifting Melly to the ground.

"I fly, Mama," laughed Melly as

Jeremiah swung her in a circle, like he always did, before putting her on the ground.

Alice laughed, too. This was a ritual Melly and Jeremiah had. She wondered if they would still be doing it when Melly wasn't such a little girl.

Melly grabbed Jeremiah's hand as she skipped down the garden path to the house.

Melly wanted Jeremiah to swing her around in a circle again, so he did.

Still smiling, Alice knocked on the door.

Sam answered and laughed at the antics of her two special people. She fingered the ring on the necklace lying warm against her skin, under her blouse. Her constant reminder of Adam and the mixed feelings she had now. Jeremiah was her husband and should have her loyalty, but Adam was her first love and part of her heart would always be with him.

She was falling in love with Jeremiah though and felt disloyal to Adam. How could she love both men? Shouldn't she remain loyal and still be in love with Adam even though he was dead, he was after all Melly's father.

His face was getting dimmer and

dimmer with each passing day. Soon, she wouldn't see his face in her mind without the picture she'd saved so Melly would know what her daddy looked like. Or was she really saving it for herself, knowing that she would forget as time passed?

"Come in, you all. Jo's just about got dinner ready."

Sam's words brought her out of her reverie and she straightened.

Jeremiah put down Melly and they all followed Sam into the house.

Jo came out of the kitchen. Tall, blonde and beautiful, she'd been a mail-order bride just like Alice, but as Alice had learned, Jo was a bounty hunter before becoming a bride.

Behind Jo stood older man who resembled Sam. Paul was Sam's father and he carried his namesake. The baby was only about three months old.

"Mama, lookit the baby."

"I see him, pumpkin. If you ask nicely maybe Paul will put him on the floor so you can play with him."

"Can I play with da baby, please?"

The older gentleman smiled. "I think that can be arranged."

Jo took a blanket from the sofa and spread it on the floor.

Grandpa Paul put baby Paul on his back on the blanket.

Melly got onto the blanket next to him.

"Hi, baby. I Melly. You little."

She tickled little Paul's belly and was rewarded with a giggle.

Alice smiled. She hoped Melly would be as gentle with her new baby brother or sister, when the time came.

"Come on into the kitchen where we can talk," said Jo, leading the way to the other room.

"I'll stay here and watch the kids," said Grandpa Paul. "Sam can fill me in later."

Sam and Jeremiah sat around the kitchen table while Alice helped Jo with dinner.

"So, you think whoever shot Walt is really after Alice? Why? Who would want to harm Alice?" asked Jeremiah, looking at his wife. He took a sip from the coffee Jo poured for him.

Sam turned in his chair and looked at Alice.

"Can you enlighten us, Alice?"

"No one." She took a deep breath then frowned. "Well, that's not entirely true. The man who murdered Adam may want to kill me as well."

"That's definitely not no one," said Sam. "Why wouldn't he have done it in New York?"

"I rarely left the house after Adam died. I suppose he didn't find an opportunity in which to do it and get away."

"So he followed you. Who is he?" asked Sam.

"His name is Dick Lane. His wife, Rebecca, went into surgery for an emergency appendectomy. Her appendix burst and I assisted but Adam couldn't save her. Mr. Lane blamed Adam and me for his wife's death. He called us murderers. Then, Adam was shot in the back when he left work one night. The police were unable to find Mr. Lane but were fairly sure it was him after what witnesses said about a man running from the scene."

"Do you think he would follow you here to Hope's Crossing?" asked Jo. She pulled a roast from the oven and set the pan on a dish towel on the counter.

"I didn't think so. I wouldn't have come here if I believed he would follow me. If I thought for a minute I'd be putting anyone in danger…"

Alice dropped into the chair next to Jeremiah, a headache pounding suddenly behind her eyes.

Jeremiah put his hand on her knee and squeezed.

"We know you wouldn't have put anyone in danger on purpose. Obviously this person has been watching us. He knew Walt was with Melly all the time. He may have even been a patient we've treated."

"The man who tried to kill me followed me here from Chicago," said Jo. "He was right under our noses all the time, but we didn't know it. I knew what he looked like, so he always stayed out of my sight, but he could have been right next to Sam or Paul, watching them and they would never have known. This is worse, because you don't know what this person looks like. Do you?"

"Vaguely." *Good grief is the mail-order bride agency cursed or is it this town?*

Alice fingered the ring on the necklace around her neck.

"He was average height, blond hair, blue eyes. He was a little on the hefty side. At that time he was clean shaven. But I don't know if I'd recognize him if I saw him again or not."

"Understood," said Sam, who straightened his back, sitting straighter in the chair. "I want you to stay inside as much as possible. I don't want you to go anywhere on your own. Even if you just go to the mercantile, take someone with you. I don't know if that will stop him, he's already shot Walt to get to you."

Alice closed her eyes, guilt for Walt's injury washed over her and she suddenly wanted to cry but she wouldn't. Not here, not now.

"I'll start canvassing for anyone who saw a blue-eyed stranger hanging about. And I'll start with the saloons."

"As bad as this sounds it's a good thing he shot Walt," said Jo. "We're forewarned this way and can make plans to keep you safe."

"We'll do whatever we need to, Sam. I just want my family protected."

His family. That's right, she was carrying his child now. Of course, he'd be more concerned with her safety.

She was worried about Melly. Her daughter could not go outside alone. Ever. At least not until this man was caught.

Above all else, she wanted Melly safe.

Jeremiah stared at her with anger in his eyes. Something was the matter, but she didn't know what had happened to change his mood so much.

*****

That night she put Melly to sleep on a pallet on the floor and then Alice undressed as usual before Jeremiah came in to bed. She took off the necklace holding Adam's wedding ring and put it on the nightstand.

"I told you not to wear that."

Alice jumped and spun to face him.

Jeremiah leaned against the door frame, arms crossed over his chest. His eyes were narrowed and his mouth formed a thin line.

She straightened her spine.

"Keep your voice down or let's take this to the kitchen." She pointed at Melly on the floor.

"The kitchen it is."

He trod out of the room, not waiting for her to follow.

Alice walked into the kitchen, her body stiff. "You can't tell me what to do. I'll stop wearing it when I'm ready. I don't wear it to bed. That should be enough for you."

He stalked across the floor and grabbed

her upper arms, giving her a little shake.

"Not wearing the damn ring to bed is not enough for me. I want everything from you. I want to fill you until there is no room in your heart for any other man."

He mashed his lips against hers, grinding them. Suddenly he softened the kiss, gentled it and pulled away enough to rest his forehead against hers.

"I'm sorry, Alice. I don't mean to hurt you. When I saw you worrying that necklace under your blouse tonight, something snapped. I was angry that you would lie to me. Now I remember that you didn't say anything when I took the necklace from around your neck."

Her body was still stiff from his onslaught. "No, I didn't, because I would never make you a promise I couldn't keep."

"And now? You're carrying my baby. Do you still carry a torch for your late husband, too."

"Perhaps, but not for the reasons you may think. Adam was my first love. He encouraged all my endeavors, from going to college to becoming a doctor. I can't forget that."

"I hope that someday you'll think of me

and not that ring."

He let her go and stomped out of the room.

Alice ran to the bedroom, collapsed on the bed, put her head in her hands and cried.

*****

A week passed. They didn't talk any more about the ring, but Alice felt the distance between them growing. Was he asking so much? Was she just being obstinate to continue wearing Adam's ring? Yes, she still loved Adam. She always would, but her feelings for Jeremiah had changed. Her love for Adam was that of a first love. Both virgins when they came together on their wedding night, they'd groped and been lucky to actually consummate the marriage that first night. They grew together.

But after knowing Jeremiah, she realized that she and Adam were woefully ignorant of what can happen between two people in love.

That was the crux of the matter. She had fallen in love with her husband, but she didn't know if he loved her in return. He talked of filling her up until there was no room in her heart for anyone but him, but he didn't say she filled his heart the same way. Maybe that's why she wasn't willing to take the ring off. She wasn't willing to put her love out there for it to be rejected, so she kept on the necklace. Kept her heart safe.

*****

The carpenters came and went day in and day out. The additions were coming along, but the noise was making her crazy. There was never anywhere to find some peace…at least during the day.

Jeremiah told her the construction would take a month, which was extremely fast, but the carpenters wanted to get it done before winter came. They would go to work in the mines during the winter so this project had to be complete.

*****

He'd almost gotten caught. After shooting the old man he'd waited, sure Alice would be the one who came to check on him, but it was her husband who came instead. Damn! And he'd brought the sheriff for good measure.

The only luck he has was that he saw them coming from a distance and could fade back into the timber and escape while they tended to the old man.

He was pretty sure they wouldn't let Walt come back here for a few days maybe weeks. She wouldn't want the old man to be alone, so things may have worked out to his benefit after all. He'd use this cabin to live in and to bring Alice to. Then he'd get her to admit her culpability in Rebecca's death before he killed her and found the peace he so needed. He'd return to Jane and raise her himself. Raise her to never forget her mother.

He ran his hand through his hair, forgetting for a moment that it was colored with boot black. His hand came away blackened, and he wiped it on his pants. He'd be glad when he didn't have to wear a disguise any longer. As soon as he could he'd take a real bath and get rid of all the grime, but for now, for just a little while longer, the masquerade was necessary.

*****

A little more than a week had passed since Walt was shot.

Alice knocked on the door of Walt's room.

With the way things were between her and Jeremiah, having Melly in their room was a blessing, that way she didn't have to come up with excuses why they couldn't make love. Although he was still so angry she doubted he wanted to make love any more than she did, which was not at all. Not with the ring, and what it represented, hanging between them.

"Come in."

"Hello, Walt. How are you doing this morning?" She put her medical bag on the floor next to the bed.

"I've been better, but all in all I'm doing just fine. How is Melly?"

Alice felt his forehead. Good no fever. "She's good. Misses you. Your color is better today. Are you up to seeing her?"

"I sure am for a little while anyway. How well am I healing, Doc Alice?"

She laughed. "Doc Alice. I like that. Sit up and let me take a look at your wound."

Walt swung his legs over the side of the bed and sat up. He wore only his pants, no shirt so Alice had easy access to his injury.

She untied the sling and removed it. Then she took off the bandages she'd put on him three days ago when she'd changed them the first time. There was a little bit of pus on the wound and an odor which she didn't like at all, but she'd take care of that.

She got the boric acid from her medical bag and poured a little on the wound.

Walt jumped a little when the liquid started bubbling.

"Hey, that tickles."

"It's supposed to. Its bubbles are cleaning away the infection on your stitches and down to where it came from. Hopefully, this will fix the problem, and I won't have to open you up and clean out the wound."

"I'm all for not needing to have another hole put in me."

She checked his pulse and found it strong. "Let me put on new bandages and the why don't you put on your shirt and come to the kitchen for breakfast. Then we'll see how you're feeling. If you're still not too tired then you can play checkers or something quiet like that with Melly."

Walt smiled and stood.

Alice got one of his clean shirts from a peg near the door and helped him put it on. She'd done the laundry so all his clothes were now clean.

"Are you still feeling okay?"

He nodded.

She'd noticed the exertion had him pale again.

"Still want to come to the kitchen? I can continue to bring you a tray up here."

"I'm good. A little sore, but that's to be expected since I got shot."

"Granpa Walt?"

Melly stood in the doorway, one hand on the door jamb, the other bunching up her skirt.

"You better now?"

He steadied himself with a hand on the back of the chair. "Ah, sweet cakes, I'm doing just fine. Your mama fixed me up good. You and I will be able to play some today. But I can't pick you up, so we'll play inside."

Melly grinned and hopped up and down, her blonde curls bouncing, her arms pumping the air around her. "Yay!"

"Okay, come on you two. Let's get some food into you, so we can begin our day."

Alice led the way, Melly and Walt walking hand-in-hand behind her. She looked back a couple of times and saw grins on both their faces.

She was just as glad they would not be outside today or any time soon. Dick Lane was still out there. Still threatening. Still wanting to kill her and maybe Melly, too.

# CHAPTER 11

September 1873

Fall was right around the corner and Alice would miss Walt's company when he went back to his cabin.

"Jeremiah." She held her coffee cup with both hands as they sat at the kitchen table before leaving for the office next door.

"Yes." He put down the medical journal he'd been reading.

"I want Walt to stay with us for the winter...maybe permanently. I don't want him to be in that cabin all by himself until spring. I've been told that the weather is not fit for man or beast at times and the snow can get so deep he couldn't get to town if he wanted to."

"That's fine. The new additions to the house and clinic will be finished by the end of the week. Walt can have a room of his own."

He cocked an eyebrow.

"Melly will have her own room again…and so will we."

"We shall." A thrill shot through her that she would be able to have relations with her husband again.

"I want you to take off that ring for good when Melly moves out. I don't want any ghosts between you and me."

She lifted her chin. "I won't be dictated to. Unless you're telling me that you love me—"

"I'm not."

"I didn't think so." Inside her heart broke a little at the finality she heard in his voice. "I'll continue to wear the ring during the day. I said I won't wear it at night and I stand by that statement."

He clinched his jaw, slapped the newspaper on the table, stood and walked away without a backward glance.

*****

September 22, 1873

The expansion of both the clinic and the house were complete. Jeremiah had two bedrooms built on the rear of the house upstairs and a library and study underneath them. The new bedrooms were a nursery and a large master bedroom for him and Alice.

The carpenters built the rooms without putting an opening into the house until the very last, so the family didn't have to put up with the sawdust.

The two clinic rooms were built on each side of the waiting room.

He stood in his new study…or was it the library? Either way what it was called didn't matter. Alice could decide which room she wanted for the library and he'd take the other.

He'd come a long way from the two-room cabin that had served as home and office when he first came to Hope's Crossing three years ago.

What was he to do with Alice? She flatly refused to take off the necklace, the wedding ring belonging to her dead husband. He wanted her to take it off and pack it away. He wouldn't make love to her until she did.

And what was that she'd said? "Unless you're saying you've fallen in love with me." How silly was that? To think they might have fallen in love with each other in such a short period of time.

He paced the room. His conscience told him the length of time didn't matter. Alice mattered. Did he love her? He liked her. A lot. She was funny and stubborn, she made him laugh and made him angry. Nothing about her was boring.

And Melly. That little one was a pip. She had kicked Jeremiah in the shin when they first met. That didn't bode well for their relationship. But he realized she was only three and she'd lost her daddy. Her mother was all she had and to her it looked like he was trying to take Alice away.

In the last few months, they'd become friends. He could truthfully say he loved her like his own child.

"Jeremiah. Are you coming in to dinner? I've fed Melly and Walt. They're reading in the living room before she goes to bed. I have our dinners in the warming shelf, but they taste better hot."

He turned at her voice. She stood only three feet from him in the doorway. So beautiful, her hands folded demurely in front of her.

"I'm coming."

She turned to go.

He stepped forward and caught her by the shoulder, stopping her.

She didn't turn to look at him but ducked her chin.

Had he broken her spirit? God, he hoped not.

"I'm sorry."

She turned and gazed up at him, her eyes swimming with tears. "So am I. I don't like to fight."

"Neither do I."

He pulled her close and cupped her face with his hands, then lowered his head and took her lips with his. A gentle kiss...he didn't want to scare her. He pressed for entrance with his tongue and she granted it. They dueled, explored and tasted each other.

She pulled back, breathing hard.

"If we were in the bedroom, I'd say skip dinner, but we're not and Walt and Melly are down in the living room and would wonder where we were."

She reached out and took his hand.

"Come with me and let's have dinner. After Melly goes to bed we can explore what we were just feeling."

"All right. You go ahead. I need to get myself under control first."

She looked down and saw the tent of his pants, gazed back up at him and smiled.

"See you shortly."

He nodded, closed his eyes and thought about taking inventory of his medical supplies. Anything to get making love to Alice off his mind. Even though the kiss resolved nothing, he couldn't stay away from her any longer. He missed her too much.

*****

He could hardly wait for dinner to be over and get Alice in his arms again. What about the necklace...her late husband's ring? She promised she wouldn't wear it at night, but he wanted her not to wear it ever. He found he wanted her to love him, to *want* to take that ring off. He knew he wasn't being fair or reasonable because he couldn't give her the love she wanted back. The more he thought about the ring, the angrier he became and anger was not the emotion he wanted at the moment.

He remembered how soft and loving she'd been before dinner. How she'd been the one to say she'd like to skip the meal and make love. Not in those exact words but with that sentiment.

Taking a deep breath, he put away his wants and thought about what he needed to do. That was to tuck in Melly and read a story in her new bedroom. He'd ordered her a new bed and let Walt have the old one. By ordering three of the same kind of bed, he'd gotten a break on the price. They were simple white iron bedsteads for Melly and for the clinic.

He walked into Melly's room where Alice was just finishing making the bed.

"I don't sleep whis you?" asked Melly her eyes round.

"No, you have your own room now," said Alice.

"Don't want own room."

Melly stamped her feet, pouted and then started to cry.

"Melly," said Jeremiah softly. "That's enough of that. You will sleep in here and if you continue to whine, you will not get a story tonight. Do you understand me?"

The little girl looked up at him, her eyes full of unshed tears. Her bottom lip quivered but she nodded her head and didn't say anything else.

Alice turned down the blankets. Then she undressed her daughter and put her in her nightgown. All through this Melly sniffled and looked up at him with sorrowful eyes.

He almost gave in. Instead he took her book of Mother Goose Nursery Rhymes off the bookshelf and sat in the chair next to her bed.

"Is Mother Goose all right for tonight?" he asked her.

She shook her head. "Cinderella."

"Okay." He returned Mother Goose to the bookshelf and picked up the Grimm Fairy Tales. When he was seated he began to read. "Once upon a time…"

*****

From the doorway, Alice watched her husband and daughter. Jeremiah was so patient with Melly and she still found it surprising, considering their first meeting. But he'd put that behind them and became the caring, but stern, father that Melly needed.

As a mother, Alice had failed since Adam's death. She'd thought of her own needs rather than Melly's, letting the child sleep with her.

Jeremiah had made that stop.

Melly was back in a room of her own.

Jeremiah read one chapter of the story before he looked down at Melly and saw she was asleep.

Alice smiled. Melly's small fit of temper had worn her out.

Jeremiah set the book on the light wood nightstand next to the bed.

"Are you ready?"

She nodded and took his hand when he held it out. Their room was no longer across the hall from Melly's but was at the end of the hall and Jeremiah had the carpenters put a lock on the door.

*He'd said, "I don't want any unexpected visitors. She can learn to knock." And I agreed with him.*

Once inside the room, he released her, turned and locked the door. Then he lit the fire that had already been set in the fireplace.

While he did so, Alice quickly slipped off the necklace and put it in her nightstand drawer.

"Now where were we this afternoon?"

He came back to her and took her in his arms.

"Ah, yes. I remember."

Lowering his head he kissed her, his

hands cradling her face. Then he moved down her neck leaving a trail of fire with each kiss.

"You took it off."

"I told you I would."

"So you did."

Did he sound a little defeated? But he didn't love her why should her wearing the necklace or not matter to him? She didn't understand, but her wearing the chain mattered a lot to him. Well, wearing it was important to her, too. Until he could tell her he loved her, why should she take off the necklace permanently?

Jeremiah didn't give her long to think. His hands moved down to her breasts and kneaded them, pinching the nipples through her clothing.

"You are wearing too many clothes," he whispered.

"So are you."

She undid the top button of his shirt and the others quickly followed.

At the same time, he released the buttons down the front of her dress, and then unhooked her corset.

"Are you planning on wearing this contraption through your pregnancy?"

"I don't know. I'd have to leave this one unfastened except for the top two hooks or buy a pregnancy corset."

"Or just leave it off all together."

She smiled.

"There is that possibility, as well…which is the one I actually prefer. I think not wearing a corset is better for the baby."

He slipped the dress down her arms, letting it hang at her waist, and then he released the rest of the hooks on the corset and dropped it to the floor. She wore a silky chemise trimmed with lace for the first time and wondered if he'd notice. The situation was almost as if she'd planned it.

He palmed her nipples, the silk rubbed against the sensitive tips. She let her head fall back, enjoying the sensation.

"You're so beautiful."

He kissed the column of her neck, then nipped it soothing the little bites with a swish of his tongue.

"Take me, Jeremiah. Take me now."

Grabbing one of the ribbons on her chemise, he pulled the bow loose, and then he quickly unlaced the garment and slid it off her arms.

He took a nipple into his mouth.

She gasped, loving the pull and wanting more.

"Alice," he breathed before switching to the other nipple.

She couldn't wait any longer; she pushed him back onto the bed, undid the rest of the buttons on her dress, untied the tape holding her bloomers and dropped both to the floor.

"Undo your pants. Now."

He wasted no time doing just what she said and freed himself.

Alice climbed up and lowered herself onto him, the fullness easing the ache she felt inside. Panting, she moved upon him, slow and then fast, as the need for completion built in her core.

Breathing heavily, she closed her eyes and felt him all the way inside her. But it wasn't enough. "Help me, Jeremiah. Help me."

"Here you go, love. Here you go."

He reached out and touched her lovebud, flicked it with his thumb and sent her to the stars.

She collapsed on his chest as he breathed her name with his completion.

They stayed like that for a moment, or an hour. She didn't know. Finally she lifted herself up off of him and walked around the bed to her side, drew down the blankets and lay on the sheets, their coolness soothing her heated body.

Jeremiah sat up, removed his boots and then his pants and underdrawers. He lay back and extended his arm toward her.

She accepted his invitation and scooted over to cuddle. That was another difference between him and Adam. They had never cuddled, she and Adam. When they had finished making love, both went to their own sides of the bed and fell asleep. She much preferred cuddling.

"I've missed you." He kissed her softly on the temple.

"And I you. I thought they'd never get the additions done."

"I must admit, I was beginning to wonder if they would ever finish but actually the time was less than the month they had quoted me."

"It seemed longer."

"Maybe because we were fighting."

"Let's not talk about that now. We've just had a wonderful respite. Can't we leave it at that for now?"

"You're right. We'll talk later."

She yawned.

"Much later."

She pulled up the blankets and covered them both.

"Goodnight, Jeremiah."

She turned over and closed her eyes.

"Goodnight, Alice. See you in the morning."

"Hmm. Morning."

Alice couldn't sleep. Adam and his ring were on her mind. How could she do this? How could she enjoy making love with Jeremiah when she should be mourning Adam? What was the matter with her? She knew the problem. She had definitely fallen in love with her husband. Each time she saw him with Melly, her heart melted. When he held her close or admired her work—so many little things made her heart flutter.

But she couldn't forget Adam. Wasn't ready to give up that part of her life, not willing to leave that love behind, when she didn't have Jeremiah's love. Yet how could he make love to her like they did and not love her? She loved him. Doubt no longer lived in her mind. That's why his not returning the emotion hurt so much.

Jeremiah reached over and pulled her back into his arms.

"Shh. I don't know why you're upset, but everything will be all right. Shh."

She accepted his comfort, though, until he spoke, she hadn't realized she was crying.

# CHAPTER 12

September 30, 1873

Four months almost five and he still hadn't gotten Alice alone. He'd had to get a job in the mine to support himself when his money ran out. Of course, he took on a fake name, Homer Johnson. Working took away from the time he could watch her and wait for her to be alone. He was limited to his time off.

He shouldn't have shot the old man. That put her on her guard. She never left the clinic on her own. Either her husband was with her or the old man and the child. He'd made a tactical error. He realized that now, but he had to be vigilant.

He decided to make his move when he saw her, the old man and the little girl leave the office. Time was running out. He had to make his move.

Dick waited in the alley between the butcher shop and the mercantile. As they passed he called out. He lay on the ground, facing the boardwalk with his eyes nearly closed, so he could see them through his eyelashes.

"Help me. Please someone help me."

"Melly, you wait right over there with Granpa Walt, while mama helps this man. Where are you injured, sir?"

He opened his eyes and sat up, his gun pointed at her.

"I'm not hurt, but you will be."

He stood.

"Come with me, Mrs. Carter or I shoot the child now."

Dick aimed the weapon at Melly.

Alice moved Melly behind her. "I'll come with you, Mr. Lane. No need to harm my daughter. And my name is Kilarney now, not Carter."

"You'll always be Carter to me. I thought you might know who I am. That saves introductions."

Suddenly, Alice knocked his arm up, pointing the gun in the air.

"Run, Melly, Walt. Run to Miss Lavernia."

Walt grabbed Melly and ran out of the alley.

As soon as they were out of sight, Alice turned and started to run after them.

Dick Lane came after her and aimed his blow to the back of her head. The butt of his gun landed with a crack and Dr. Alice Carter folded into a heap on the ground. He picked her up and threw her over his shoulder, ran down the alley to his horse and laid her over the saddle. Then he climbed up behind and kicked the horse into a canter.

He headed out of town to the old man's cabin where he'd been living these past months. She didn't regain consciousness, even as he carried her inside and put her on the bed.

Dick tied her right wrist to her right ankle. She wasn't going anywhere.

Then he made a pot of coffee. The aroma of the fresh brew must have brought her around because she opened her eyes at last.

*****

Alice blinked several times before her surroundings came into focus. She didn't know where she was only that her head hurt terribly. When she tried to reach up and touch her head, she discovered her predicament. And what about her baby, how did he get her here? She didn't remember seeing anything but a horse. No wagon in the alley, which meant she was slung over the saddle.

*Melly! Where is Melly?*

She looked around the cabin and didn't see her daughter anywhere. Walt must have gotten her away.

"Oww."

"'bout time you came to. Would you like a cup of coffee?"

She felt the rope around her wrist and ankle. "Wh…what? Why are you being nice to me? You're planning on killing me, aren't you?"

"Of course, but that's no reason to not be civil. I want something from you that you're more likely to give me if I'm nice."

Her heart pounded in her chest. This man was cold and calculating, yet he'd taken quite a risk taking her as he had. That made him even more dangerous. She must stay focused and not panic. Keeping herself calm also meant staying alive.

"You're a strange man, Mr. Lane. There is no way I can drink a cup of coffee in this condition. I can't even sit up."

He moved over to her and pulled a great, long knife from his boot.

She inadvertently cringed and pulled back.

"Just so you are aware, if you throw the coffee at me I will tie you up and you will not be comfortable. Am I clear?"

She nodded. "Perfectly."

He cut the rope that tied her, then took the coffee over and handed her the cup.

Hands shaking she took the cup and sloshed some of the steaming brew over the side onto her skirt. The cabin was cold which made her shake even more.

He must have felt the chill too, because he built a fire in the fireplace and lit it with a long match from the box on the mantle.

"Wh…where are we?"

"Don't you recognize the place? This is your friend Walt's cabin."

"Why would I recognize it? I've never been here before."

"That's right. Your husband and the sheriff came to check on the old man when he didn't show up the day I shot him. All-in-all this place has worked out best for me. I needed an out-of-the-way place to bring you...once I caught you. This is the perfect place."

"What will killing me achieve? It won't bring your wife back."

"Her name was Rebecca, and I will have my vengeance. Satisfaction. Peace of mind, once you're dead, too."

"Peace of mind? You think I killed your wife, but the truth of the matter is she was already dead when you brought her in. Her appendix had ruptured, spreading the poison into her body. Adam and I did our best but it was too late."

"No. That's not true. It can't be true."

"But it is. If we'd gotten to her sooner, perhaps we could have saved her, but even then it may not have helped."

"No. You're lying. She just had a stomach ache. That's all. And you killed her."

At that moment, the sound of horses hooves galloping up to the cabin made him turn. He went to the window.

"You have the luck of the Irish, Dr. Alice Carter. That's your new husband and the sheriff...again. Afraid I have to go."

He ran out the back door.

She ran after him and, through the open door, watched him mount a brown horse with four white socks and ride into the forest.

The front door smashed open. Sam Longworth, gun drawn, came through followed by Jeremiah.

She pointed at the open door. "He ran out the back."

Jeremiah hurried close and gathered her in his arms.

"Are you all right?"

"I'm fine. What about Melly? Is she safe?"

"She's all right. She's with Walt. He'll protect her with his life, you know that."

She nodded and put her hand to her throat, taking a deep breath. "Walt did. He saved my little girl. Got her away while I occupied Dick Lane.

"Lane was so strange. He gave me a cup of coffee and said he wanted something from me. The situation was like we were friends having afternoon tea."

"Look at me," commanded Jeremiah.

She looked up at him.

"What?"

"Your eyes are dilated. Did he hit you?"

"Yes. I didn't come around until we got here. My head is pounding, has been since I regained consciousness. I probably have a concussion, but I'll be fine."

"You're not fine. Let me take you home."

Sam came back inside.

"He's gone. Neither hide nor hair in sight."

"He's been staying here since he shot Walt," said Alice. "And he's got black hair. I never would have recognized him."

"Will you now?" asked Sam.

She nodded. "Yes, I think so. I got a pretty good look at him. Although if he changes his hair color and shaves off his beard, I may not."

"That's all right," said Sam as he holstered his pistol. "He's getting desperate. After waiting all this time to capture you and then to lose you, he'll try again and we'll catch him. Don't worry, he won't evade me forever. He'll make a fatal mistake and he will be mine."

*****

Sam lifted Alice onto Jeremiah's lap for the ride home. She wasn't very big and didn't know how to ride a horse. Besides Jeremiah liked the feel of her safe in his arms.

For her part, she cuddled into him like he was a blanket and she couldn't get warm. She shivered against him, not from cold he knew, but from fear. He kept both arms around her while holding the reins with his hands.

"You're safe now Alice. Melly is safe. Why do you shiver so?"

"He got away and can still come back. Until he's captured or killed Melly and I are in danger. We should leave. Our being here puts you in danger, too and it has already gotten Walt shot, just because he knows us. We should have left then, but I was too busy."

"No."

"No, what?" She leaned back in his arms and looked up at him.

"No. You're not leaving. You'll put yourself and Melly at greater risk, and I won't have that. You are *my* wife. You'll *stay* my wife, which means being here with me."

He felt her relax. She needed to hear that he wanted her to stay. She probably wouldn't even have thought of leaving if he'd told her he loved her, but he couldn't say something he was unsure of. As long as she wore that damnable ring, she couldn't really love him could she? He'd be damned if he loved her without the possibility of her returning the emotion. He...he couldn't...refused...

He clasped her tighter. Who was he kidding? He'd fallen in love with her sometime ago. When he saw how gentle she was with the patients, especially the children, he fell a little for her. And the emotion kept building. He wanted to give her everything she desired. That's why he'd put the additions on the house and clinic. Made it a real clinic, almost a hospital, at least as far as Hope's Crossing was concerned. She'd wanted the changes, and he wanted to give them to her.

They finally reached town, and Jeremiah pulled the horse to a stop on the side of the house behind the clinic. He helped her down before dismounting himself.

Rather than go inside, Alice waited for him.

"You should go in...see Melly...warm up."

"Probably, but I want to stay with you."

"I'm just putting the horse back in the barn. I'll be in shortly."

She still didn't move.

"Alice. What is it?"

"I'm afraid for you. I don't want you out of my sight."

"It's not me he wants. It's you. I'm fairly safe. Now go on inside."

She looked at the house and then back to him.

"If you're sure."

"I am. Go kiss Melly and tell her how much we love her."

Alice cocked her head and looked at him like she'd never seen him before. Her eyebrows where furrowed in concentration and her full lips were in a slight frown. "You really do."

"Do what?"

"Love her. You love my daughter."

"Our daughter, and yes, I do."

He wrapped the reins around the hitching rail and walked over to Alice taking her in his arms and hugging her tightly. Or as tightly as he could with her expanding belly.

"You worry too much and that is not

good for our son."

She smiled as he wanted.

"What makes you think this baby is not a girl?"

"Because we already have a daughter. It is time for a son."

"I like that you said *we* have a daughter."

"Melly is our daughter and, whether she likes it or not, I am her daddy. I love her, Alice, just as much as if she were my own blood. That doesn't matter to me. She's my daughter."

He looked down at his little wife.

She gazed up at him with tears in her eyes.

"Ah, you're not going to cry are you?"

"No." The first tear rolled down her cheek, followed by all its friends. Soon her cheeks were wet from her tears.

He sighed and held her close, letting her cry, getting out the fear.

She sniffled a little and pulled a handkerchief from her sleeve, to dab at the corners of her eyes and at her cheeks, removing the last of her tears.

"Better?"

"Yes. Thank you. I've gotten a hold of

myself and need to see my...our daughter. I need to have her in my arms."

He understood that need. He'd had the same feeling but for Alice, since he already knew Melly was safe with Walt. Jeremiah wasn't stretching the truth when he said the old man would die for the little girl. Walt loved her more than anyone else. He'd grown fond of Jeremiah and Alice, of that there was no doubt, but Melly was the most important person in his life.

Jeremiah wondered what the both of them would think of the new baby, less than five months away from being born. He wasn't too worried about it. They would love the baby. Melly would be disappointed that she couldn't play with him yet, Walt would be afraid to touch him because he was so small but both of them would love the baby.

Now he just had to keep Alice safe. The man after her was crazy enough to follow her from New York City just to exact revenge. That's a long way to come and he'd been a patient man so far, waiting until he could find Alice without minimal escort. Would he wait again or would he be more brazen. That was what worried Jeremiah.

What if the man came to the clinic and Alice was the one to treat him? If he got her alone, what would he do now?

*****

That was close. Too close. He needed a new plan? She would recognize him with the black in his hair and with the beard. Time to go in disguise…as himself. He didn't believe that Dr. Alice Carter remembered him now. She knew him only because she'd been expecting him. Who else would kidnap her? But if he shaved the beard *and* the hair, not even his own mother would recognize him.

He laughed and headed for the bath house. Time to get clean. Then he would put his new plan into effect.

# CHAPTER 13

October 1873

More than five months into her pregnancy and she was tearier than ever. She didn't remember being this way with Melly, which was another reason she thought this baby must be a boy. She had less than four months to go and already she was anticipating the birth. On top of that here it was October and she hadn't finished her Christmas presents. She would have to break down and buy some if she didn't start knitting faster.

Alice had new clothes made for Melly. She was growing so fast nothing was fit for very long. Alice saved the clothes though. They'd get used by another of her daughters or maybe Jo's. She had been kind to Alice from the beginning and become her friend over the months.

"Mister," she looked down at the sign in sheet. "Bitmore. Mr. Ezra Bitmore?"

A tall, husky man with black wool coat, brown wool pants and black bowler hat spoke but didn't stand.

"That's me."

"If you'll come with me, Mr. Bitmore, I'll take care of you."

"I want to see the man doctor."

"I'm sorry Mr. Bitmore, he's unavailable." She was glad Jeremiah was in number one.

He looked at the floor, shook his shaggy head and stood.

"All right. You can do it."

"Thank you. I'll do my best."

Alice was cringing inside. She was so tired of having to prove herself every single day to someone.

She let the man back to examination room number two.

"What is your problem today, Mr. Bitmore?"

"I got pain in my chest. When my da got pain like this, he died. Had a heart attack and died. I don't want to die. Fix me!"

With every word he got louder until the last two where a shout.

"Calm down, sir. I need to listen to your heart." She waved a hand toward his outer garment. "Please remove your coat and sit on the table."

Once his coat was off she understood why he'd kept it on inside. The man's threadbare shirt had holes in the elbows that showed his red long underwear. He sat on the table and loomed over her. She had to remind herself he was just a patient.

Alice took her stethoscope and pressed it to the upper chest on the right side of his back.

"Take a deep breath."

She moved the instrument to the left side.

"Again, please."

And so it went as she listened to the lower lungs, as well. Then she listened to the front of his lungs.

"Have you been coughing and did you expectorate anything?"

"Did I what?"

"Did you cough anything up and if you did what color was it?"

"Well, yeah." He stopped and coughed.

"It's been green and thick. From my nose, I figure."

"Well part of the discharge is sinus drainage, but I believe you have pneumonia. This can be very serious, and you need to be in bed, drinking willow bark tea—"

"I don't have pneumonia," he shouted and stood. "I tell you, I'm having a heart attack. Where is the doc? The real doc?"

Alice didn't step back at his shouting. No one would intimidate her about medicine.

The door slammed open as Jeremiah entered. "What is happening in here? What is the shouting about?"

"Mr. Bitmore has pneumonia and doesn't believe me. He's diagnosed himself as having a heart attack."

"Sit down, Bitmore. Let me listen to you."

Jeremiah performed the same examination that Alice had and asked the same questions.

"You have pneumonia, Bitmore. You need to be in bed and taking willow bark tea for pain, which I'm sure is what my wife told you."

Bitmore hung his head and then raised it

again. "Yeah, that is what she said to do. But she's a woman. What does she know about doctoring?"

"More than I do, so consider yourself lucky you got to see her."

"Yes, sir. I will from now on."

"Now," said Alice. "Go to the mercantile, tell Lavernia to sell you some willow bark and then go home and make the tea. Drink lots of liquids. Only take a cup of tea every four hours. Water is best, then broth. If you try to work before this infection is gone, you'll get sick again and may die. Do you understand?"

"Yes, Dr. ma'am. I'm sorry, Dr. Kilarney, ma'am."

"I accept your apology, Mr. Bitmore. Just go home and take care of yourself."

"Yes, Dr. ma'am."

He scooted off the table and hurried out of the room shutting the door behind him.

"Thank you for agreeing with my evaluation," she said to Jeremiah as she wrote notes in a file.

"There was no reason to disagree. You were correct in your diagnosis."

He stuffed his stethoscope into his pocket and wrapped an arm around her shoulder. Then he placed a hand on her belly and talked to the baby.

"Are you kicking your father today?"

He moved his hand around and suddenly stopped.

She felt the baby kick him and then move away.

"You're bothering *her*." She loved to tease him and disagreed just to do so.

"I know. *He's* a strong one."

"Are you excited Jeremiah? To become a father of a baby for the first time? Babies are so different when they are brand new."

He took hold of her other shoulder and faced her. "I know. I've brought plenty of them into this world. I'll bring this one, and every other baby we have, into the world, too. Are you scared? Because I won't let anything happen to you or the babies."

She looked into his gray eyes and felt warmth in her chest at the protective look on his face. "I know you won't, but I also know the statistics."

He pulled her in for a hug. "Damn the statistics. I haven't lost a mother or baby yet, and I don't intend to start now."

She smiled. His vehemence soothed her. Not that she was afraid, but being a doctor, she did know that nearly one in five mothers or babies died in childbirth. So many variables were involved...was the mother healthy, was the baby turned correctly, was it the mother's first pregnancy, and too many others to name. She was sure that she would be fine and her baby was strong and healthy, just as Melly had been.

She'd never let Jeremiah know it, but she hoped this baby was a son. He was right; they already had a daughter that they loved beyond measure. A son would complete their little family...for now. She was sure there would be more babies in the future, but for now, they would be a perfect family.

\*\*\*\*\*

November 1, 1873

Alice pulled the ham from the oven. She'd dotted it with cloves and glazed it with honey and now the wonderful aroma made her mouth water. Scalloped potatoes were ready in the warmer and fresh baked dinner rolls were on the counter. A jar of green beans and one of corn completed the main meal. For dessert she'd made an apple pie with canned apples. All the canned goods were gifts or payments from patients.

She certainly didn't have the time or the skills to can food herself.

Melly turned four today and this was her birthday celebration.

Alice was six months pregnant. This pregnancy was different in so many ways. She seemed to be more tired than she remembered being with Melly, but she hadn't been working with Melly.

Now while the ham rested they would open presents.

She went into the living room. "Come on everyone. Let's watch Melly open her presents."

Melly ran down the stairs followed by Walt.

Jeremiah came down from his study. Even on his days off he worked. Reading his books and journals on the latest medical findings.

"Melly, are you ready to open your presents?"

She cocked her head and put her hand on her hip. "Mama, I is four-years-old. I not a baby."

Alice smiled. Jeremiah and Walt both chuckled quietly less the little fireball turn her gaze their way.

The three adults watched Melly open her presents. First she opened the new doll from Mama and Doc.

"A dolly!"

She hugged the doll to her body and danced around in circles.

"What do you say to Doc?"

"Thanks, Doc."

She walked over and gave him a kiss on the cheek.

Alice smiled. Her baby girl and Jeremiah had come a long way together, and Alice was pleased over their relationship. She might still call him 'Doc' but when she was ready Alice was sure Melly would call him daddy.

"And thank you, too, Mama."

Melly gave Alice a kiss, too.

Grandpa Walt gave Melly a new box of crayons.

"Walt, how did you get those?" Alice pointed at the colorful box containing the crayons. "What a wonderful gift. I had to get them from Aunt Tilly in London."

He shrugged. "I found them in one of them catalogs Lavernia gets. Ordered them months ago so I'd be sure to have them for today."

Melly jumped up and down with excitement.

"Thank you, Granpa Walt. Now we can color lots more."

"That's right, sweet cakes. We can color whatever we want to."

After Melly opened all of her presents, it was time for dinner.

Alice stood and led everyone to the kitchen. When everyone had sat, she said grace.

"Thank you, Lord, for these many blessings we have received throughout the year. Thank you especially for our family and friends. Amen."

*****

Mid November 1873

He approached the clinic door. His hands sweated, and he wiped one of them on his pants. He'd bought new pants at the mercantile a couple of months before and worn them all the time, sleeping and bathing included, wanting to get them worn looking before he continued his quest to kill Alice Carter. He'd also bought a new shirt, coat and bowler hat. The purchases had taken the rest of the money he had brought with him.

He had to survive on the money he made at the mine, now.

He wore nothing that she might recognize from before except his boots. He spit-shined them but he didn't want to break in a new pair. He couldn't see the point of spending the money when it was unlikely she'd paid any attention to what he'd worn on his feet. The feeling of being clean for the first time in months had been wonderful and he savored it. He'd bathed every week since then and shaved his head and face every day.

Going to the clinic was a big gamble. What if she recognized him? He'd had to have a reason to see them, so he took his knife and stabbed his left hand enough to need stitches. The act had hurt like hell, but would be worth it if…no make that *when*…he got the lady doctor alone to see if she knew him. And he could check out the clinic for escape routes. For now he had the wounded hand wrapped in a dirty handkerchief. That was all he had to wrap it in and thought it would provoke sympathy from the lady doctor. He took his hat off and set it in his lap, covering his hand.

"Mr. Johnson."

Alice Carter—no it was Kilarney now—called the name he was using. He looked up.

She smiled at him.

He lowered his voice and growled. "That'd be me."

"What is your problem today?"

"Cut myself whittling."

"Please follow me."

She took him into an examination room.

"Please sit on the table and I'll get your injury taken care of quickly."

He complied with her request. Dick figured he needed to get the wound taken care of anyway.

"Can you remove the bandage, please? Or would you rather that I did?"

"I can."

He slowly unwrapped his hand revealing a red, angry wound.

"Oh, my. That'll require stitches. I'll first need to wash your hand and make sure the wound is a clean as possible."

She walked to the counter where a pitcher and basin sat. After pouring water into the basin she picked up the bowl, a washcloth and bar of soap and brought them back to where he sat.

Alice—he could think of her as Alice

now after all they'd been through together—set the things on the table and placed the washcloth in the water. After wringing it out, she rubbed the bar of soap into the cloth, then she took his hand and gently cleansed around the wound.

He was surprised at her tenderness. No doctor he'd had before had been gentle with him. Suddenly, he saw Rebecca in his mind and wondered if this doctor had been as kind to her. No. He couldn't start thinking of her like that. He had to kill her. He had to finish it. For Rebecca.

"There, that's better. Now I'm putting some boric acid on the wound and with a wound as deep as yours the liquid is likely to hurt, but it will help prevent any infection from forming."

"Just do what you got to, Dr. Kilarney."

He gritted his teeth and nearly screamed when she poured the liquid into the wound.

"Okay now, let me stitch you up and then you'll be good to go."

She put ten stitches in his hand and covered the wound with a white bandage.

"Keep the bandage dry and try not to get it dirty. If you have to work with it, wear your gloves…and no whittling."

"Yes, ma'am. When do I come back to get the stitches out?"

"Come see me in ten days. I'll remove them then."

He slid off the table.

"What do I owe you?"

"One dollar for today and that will take care of the next visit, as well."

"Thanks, Doc."

"You're welcome. I wish all my patients were as easy to work on as you."

He smiled. She had no idea who he was and his visit today had proved his new disguise worked and told him that the only way out was through the front door or the house the clinic was attached to.

Now he had ten days to figure out how to kill her. Ten days before Dr. Alice Carter Kilarney would pay with her life for taking his true love. But first he'd get the answers he needed for his peace of mind.

*****

Walking slow, her back hurting, Alice blew out the lamp and closed the curtains in examination room one, then walked across the hall and did the same with room two. The windows were high on the wall so they provided light without sacrificing privacy for the patients.

Jeremiah was still in the surgery with a patient but they had no overnight patients, thank God.

She rubbed her aching back and the movement irritated her baby, who dutifully kicked her. Alice put her hand on her belly.

"It's all right little one. You'll be here soon enough. Just a few more weeks."

"Is my son giving you troubles?" Jeremiah walked up beside her.

"Your *daughter* makes a habit of giving her mother trouble. Is your patient gone?"

"Yes, and I closed and locked the door."

She rubbed her belly. "I'm beginning to think you might be right about this child being a boy. Melly was never this much trouble."

Jeremiah grinned like the proud papa he was, which for some unknown reason annoyed her.

"Does his being a brat all-ready make you happy?"

"I think he's just getting ready to be born."

"Well," she let out a sigh. "It cannot be too soon for me. I'm tired of having an aching back and swollen feet."

Jeremiah took her in his arms and held her as close as possible.

Too close, as far as the baby was concerned. The child kicked and moved like she was trying to push her father away.

"I don't think she likes you."

"Too bad. He'll have to get used to me."

"I'll be glad when this child is born, and we know its gender. I'm tired of correcting you."

He threw back his head and laughed.

"You'll miss the sparing we do. I know you. You like to argue."

She jutted out her chin. "I do not."

"See."

"Oh, pooh."

He laughed again and then kissed her.

She softened as his lips moved over hers.

"Come." He released her. "Let's go see what kind of mischief Walt and Melly are up to."

They walked through the clinic to where it attached to the kitchen of their home. Sitting at the table was Grandpa Walt and their now four-year-old daughter Melly. They each had a cup in front of them.

"What are you two up to?"

"Granpa Walt made us hot cocoa 'cause I beated him."

"You beat him? At what?" asked Alice. She looked at the table for a game.

"We made a snowman and I got my snow ball done first."

"Sss…sno…snowman?"

Alarm coursed through Alice.

"Now, Alice, she needs to have some fresh air," said Walt. "We stayed in the front yard where everyone could see us, so there was no danger."

Her body stiffened, her back ramrod straight. "You don't know that, Walt. You had no right to take her outside. What if something happened? What if…"

She couldn't go on, her breathing was too fast. She felt herself starting to fall.

"Alice!"

Jeremiah was there, lifting her in his arms and carrying her to the sofa in the living room.

"Do *not* move," he said as he laid her down.

"Mama?"

"Keep her back, Walt. I need to examine Alice."

He knelt next to the sofa, took his

stethoscope from his pocket and listened to her heart.

"You're heart is beating a mile a minute. You need to calm down."

Then he listened to her lungs.

"Breathe. That's right. Again. Breathe."

Alice closed her eyes and saw Dick Lane carrying off Melly, Walt lying on the snow-covered ground, a bright red pool spreading from his head, in stark contrast to the white beside him.

"No!" She opened her eyes.

"I'm sorry, Alice," said Walt.

He held Melly's hand keeping her back, away from her parents.

Alice breathed slower and slower, calming herself.

"I shouldn't have reacted like that. Just please, please don't take her outside without letting me know."

"I won't. I'm so sorry."

"It's all right, Walt. Take Melly and go finish your cocoa before it gets cold."

"Yes, *ma'am*."

She heard the anger in his voice but it didn't matter. Melly's safety mattered.

After they'd gone. Alice broke into tears. She put her arm over her eyes to quell the onslaught of salty liquid streaming from her eyes.

After a minute or so, she held her arms out. "Help me up, please."

"Certainly," said Jeremiah.

He grasped her hands, pulled her to a sitting position, then he sat down next to her and put an arm around her shoulders.

"Do you feel better?"

"Yes. The visions I had in my mind." She shook her head to clear it. "I panicked. I shouldn't have done that. We've been safe these months. Maybe he went away…"

"We must remain vigilant…but…we also cannot let this man run our lives. We cannot live in fear. Melly needs to do the things that little girls do and that includes making snowmen with Grandpa Walt."

"You're right. I know you are. But I'm still afraid. I don't know how to get past my fear."

"I can only tell you I will do my best to keep you safe. I won't leave you alone. If you want we'll start seeing patients together."

"No. Being a doctor in the clinic is one place I do feel safe. I can't imagine that he would come into the clinic."

"You're probably right. And as you said, nothing has happened in months. More than likely he's left town."

"I know. Let's go have dinner. I prepared a stew earlier and Walt has been watching it all day. I'll make biscuits and we'll have a meal."

"Sounds great, but Mr. Valdez brought in two loaves of fresh bread as payment for today. They're on the counter in the kitchen. You don't have to make biscuits."

"Oh, that's wonderful. I'm really too tired to make biscuits, anyway."

She led the way to the kitchen.

Alice walked immediately to Walt and hugged him.

"You were right, Walt. I was wrong to react that way. Melly does need fresh air and to be able to play. As long as it's in the front yard, I don't see any problem. Thank you. Thank you for loving my daughter so."

Walt looked up, tears filling his eyes.

"I ain't got no other family. I couldn't love any of you more, especially this little tadpole."

He rubbed Melly's head.

"We love you, too," said Alice and hugged him again.

"Now let's eat that stew you've watched for me all day. How's it look?"

"Great," said Walt. "I just checked it when we came in and you outdid yourself this time. It looks perfect."

"I'm sure that has more to do with your taking care of it all day than me putting it together."

"I don't care who's responsible for the stew. I just want to eat it," complained Jeremiah.

"All right. Will you get the stew, please. I see that Walt and Melly have already set the table."

Jeremiah got the Dutch oven full of stew and set it on a towel in the middle of the table.

Alice took the ladle and served Melly first putting just one ladle full in her bowl. Then she buttered a piece of bread and gave it to her.

She said, "Let's eat, gentlemen."

They held hands to say grace and then Jeremiah served all the adults a full bowl of the still simmering dish.

Everyone was hungry, even Melly, and they ate in silence for a few minutes.

"Mama, why you mad at Granpa Walt?"

Finally it was Melly who broke the silence.

"I'm not mad at him, sweetheart. I was just scared for a minute."

"Why you scared?"

*How am I to explain this to her?*

"Some men in the world are bad. I just want to make sure everyone is safe."

"Bad men hurts us?"

"Yes. The bad men will hurt us."

"I fight the bad men."

"You will, huh?" said Alice with a smile.

Melly nodded vigorously. "I not let bad men hurts us."

"Thank you, sweetheart. I feel much better knowing you will keep us safe."

"Yup. I pertect you."

"Protect. You will protect us."

"Yup. That's what I say."

Alice laughed. "So you did."

*If only it were so easy. If only I knew what to expect and when, then I'd know how to keep us safe. God, I wish I knew.*

# CHAPTER 14

"No! No! Not Melly. Please not my baby!" Alice thrashed, kicking out, pulling the blankets off onto the floor

"Alice. Alice!"

"Jeremiah?"

"You're having a nightmare."

He pulled her into his arms, her back to his chest.

"It's all right. You're safe. Melly is safe."

Breathing hard, Alice broke into tears.

"He had her. He was taking her away."

"Hush, now. It was just a dream. Nothing more. Shh. I've got you."

"Why do you do this to yourself? You could just let us go. You don't love me anyway."

"You're my wife, Melly is my daughter

and you're about to have my son. I'm never letting any of you go. You all belong to me." Then he added, quietly, "You still wear his ring around your neck. I haven't got a chance against the love you still bear him."

"Or daughter."

"What?" He stiffened and tightened his hold on her.

"Son or daughter."

"Well, you must feel better. You're sparring with me."

She didn't really feel better, but worse, yet she smiled. Even though he couldn't see her, she was sure he felt her smile. She had to or she just might start crying again. As much as she wanted him to say that he loved her, holding her while she cried, telling her that they were his, was almost as good, and she'd take those feelings for now. One day she hoped he'd realize that he loved her and would be able to tell her. Until then, she'd always hold a bit of herself back from him. A small piece of her heart that couldn't be broken.

*****

The day had come. Time to get the stitches out of his hand and finish what he came to Montana to do. Kill Alice Carter.

Doing the deed was so hard though. She was expecting, and the thought of killing a woman in the family way was somehow repugnant. But, he had to. He'd promised himself, and Rebecca.

His conscience told him he was wrong. Rebecca wouldn't want this, but how was he to go on without Rebecca if he didn't kill Alice? How would he find peace of mind, if she lived? Why should she be allowed to live? Why?

Dick rubbed his hands over his freshly shaved head as the frustration of the situation rained over him.

He didn't know what he would do. Suddenly, he questioned what he believed— all the time—the planning. Was he wrong? Is that why killing Dr. Adam Carter had brought no relief? Why he still grieved so deeply?

Dick sat on the bed in the small room he rented, with his head down and his hands hanging between his knees as the tears fell to the plain wood floor.

*****

Alice couldn't get the dream out of her mind and it left her skittish while working in the clinic. She was determined not to let her irrational fear rule her life or affect the way she cared for her patients.

"Mr. Johnson. Mr. Homer Johnson," she read the name off the sign-in sheet and glanced around the waiting room.

"Here."

His voice sounded even more gravelly than it had the last time.

Alice smiled.

"Have you gotten a cold, Mr. Johnson? Your voice sounds a bit hoarse."

"Maybe a little bit of one."

"If it was summer I'd tell you to eat rose hips, but I doubt you can find any this time of year. Instead, I suggest you drink hot tea with honey and a good measure of whiskey. That should soothe your throat and any cough you may have."

"Thank you." He narrowed his eyes. "Why are you bein' so nice to me?"

*That's a very odd question.* "I'm a doctor. I try to treat all my patients with dignity and concern. I want you healthy more than anything. Nothing would make me happier than to find that my services are no longer needed. Follow me to an examination room, please."

He followed her.

"Please get on the table and let me see your hand. "

He lifted his hand toward her and she unwrapped the bandages. The wound looked a little pink but otherwise completely healthy.

"You've done a great job with this. Let me get those stitches out for you and you'll be right as rain."

"I don't want to like you. I can't like you. You have to die," he whispered the words so she could barely hear them.

"I'll be right back. I have to get my scissors from the other room."

Alice left the room, her heart pounding in her chest. Could that be Dick Lane? Why else would he say those things?

She hurried down the hall to the surgery where Jeremiah was setting a broken arm on the Murphy's youngest boy.

"Jeremiah! Jeremiah! He's here," she whispered it, afraid the man in the room down the hall would hear her.

He looked up from his patient. His eyebrows furrowed. "Who? Who's here?"

"Lane. Dick Lane is in my exam room."

"Calm down, now. Calm down."

He placed his hands on Alice's

shoulders.

"What makes you think this man is Dick Lane?"

She shuddered. "He said he didn't want to like me. That he needs to kill me. He whispered the words like he was talking to himself."

"All right you stay here with Timmy, and I'll go see this person."

She nodded and glanced at Timmy.

"The cast looks done, is that right?"

"Yes, he just needs a sling."

"I can do that."

She placed her hand on Jeremiah's arm.

"Be careful."

"I will. Just take care of Timmy."

He left the room.

Although her thoughts raced, she picked up a large square of cloth and folded it in half. She tied the cloth around the boy's neck and had Timmy place his arm in the sling.

"You wear this for the next six weeks. Then come back and see either me or Dr. Kilarney. Most likely your cast will come off and you won't need the sling, either."

The red-haired boy fidgeted on the table. "Yes ma'am. Can I go now?"

"Not until Dr. Kilarney returns and says that you can."

No sooner had the words left her mouth, Jeremiah returned.

"Well?" asked Alice.

Jeremiah checked over Timmy. "You can go now. Remember to wear the sling all the time. Okay?"

"Yes, sir."

Timmy slipped off the table and out of the room.

"I checked the exam room and the waiting room. Lane is nowhere to be seen. He's gone, must have heard you come over here or decided you'd been gone too long or something. Anyway, he's gone."

Relief washed through her, immediately replaced by new fear. She paced the room. "What about Melly?"

"Walt is with her. She's fine."

Again the relief was palpable.

"He said something about not wanting to like me."

"Perhaps that's it. It's like Androcles and the lion. You were kind to him. Once he got to know you and saw how you treated your patients, he liked you and didn't want to kill you any longer."

"Or he could have been afraid he'd get caught," said Alice, a shiver working its way up her spine. "I treated him ten days ago and didn't recognize him."

"We weren't sure you'd know him if you saw him. He's obviously changed his appearance drastically or you would have."

She pointed to her own head. "He did. He shaved his beard and his head. His clothes were different and so was his hat. Oh, God, Jeremiah, what am I to do?"

"Nothing. He had the opportunity twice and didn't do it, but just to be safe from now on, you will see only the female patients. Then he has no chance to fool us again and get to you."

Jeremiah put his arms around her and hugged her close. Even the baby didn't seem to mind today.

"Are you sure you wouldn't rather take the day off and go rest? I don't want you to exert yourself needlessly."

"No, I'm fine. I'll just fret if I can't work. Better to stay busy and keep my mind off what just happened."

"We need to let Sam know. I'll send Walt. Instead of working you take the time to play with or read to Melly, so she won't want to go with Walt. I'll handle what patients we have left."

She paused for a moment. "All right. You're suggestion is the most logical."

She tried to keep the tremor out of her voice but didn't succeed.

He rubbed her back and held her close.

"Everything will be fine. You'll see. Play with Melly. Taking some time and playing with our daughter will be good for you both. Walt is good with her and for her, but there is nothing like having Mama play with you."

She nodded against his chest. Feeling him gave her comfort. His arms wrapped around her like a protective blanket and he soothed her.

Arm in arm, they went back out to the waiting room.

The last patients had been Timmy and his mother.

She looked over to the corner and saw Walt sitting against the wall with his head down. Melly was nowhere to be seen.

"Melly! Where is Melly?"

Jeremiah ran to Walt. He lifted Walt's chin and saw that he'd been knocked out.

"Walt. Walt! Wake up, man."

He slapped the older man.

"Alice, get me some water."

Heart pounding, she shuffled back to the examination room as fast as she could and brought back the pitcher and a towel. She handed both to Jeremiah.

He took the pitcher and tossed the contents into Walt's face.

The man sputtered and opened his eyes.

"Where is Melly?"

Jeremiah shook Walt.

"Where is Melly?"

"He musta taken her."

"Who? Who took her?"

"The bald man. I was sittin' here playin' checkers with Melly and losin' as usual, when this man came up to us. I could tell he was bald, even though he were a wearin' a bowler hat. He said he had a little girl about Melly's age and he sure missed her. I looked over at Melly and that's the last thing I remember."

"I'm getting Sam," said Jeremiah.

"I'll come with you," said Walt.

"No. I want you to stay here and let Alice look you over. Then the both of you lock this office and go into the house. I'll be back shortly."

"I want to come with you," said Alice as she bit her fingernails.

"No. You need to stay here. I don't need you having the baby in the middle of the street because you overexerted yourself. I'll find Melly and bring her home."

He kissed her.

"I promise. Now, lock the door behind me."

Jeremiah left.

Alice and Walt went back to the house and stayed in the kitchen. That's where the side door to the outside was and where Jeremiah would be returning. She made a pot of coffee for something to do. Then she sat at the table. Then she paced the floor from the door to the table and back again.

Darkness was closing in on them when Jeremiah left. Now night had completely fallen and there was no sign of Jeremiah or Sam.

"I'm going crazy," said Alice. "I want to go after Jeremiah but I know I can't."

"That's right you're waiting here with me just like Doc said. I'm sorry, Alice. I guess I'm not too good at keeping Melly safe after all."

"Walt, you couldn't help it. He knocked

you out."

"I shoulda known somethin' was off when he came out of the room in such a hurry. But I didn't think nothin' about it."

"You couldn't have known who he was. I didn't at first. If he hadn't said the things he did, I wouldn't have known."

"Why'd he take Melly?"

"He wants me. He knows I'll do anything for her."

"That's right I do."

The gravelly voice emanated from the doorway into the living room. Dick Lane stood there with Melly in his arms. Then he walked into the middle of the kitchen floor.

"I couldn't go too far with her, she would have put up a fight and maybe screamed, but she's a good girl. Aren't you, Melissa?"

"I'm Melly. Put me down!"

*Her daughter.* Her Melly was pounding her little hands on Dick Lane's bare head.

He kept trying to catch her hands but couldn't. Finally, he shook her.

"Be still."

"Put me down!"

Melly screamed and kicked and wiggled. Blood pounding. Alice jumped to her feet and ran at him. She kicked him in the shins and scratched his face.

"Stop that," he yelled.

He dropped Melly and pushed Alice away.

She fell back, landing on her backside. Her hands cradled her belly.

Dick Lane loomed over Alice.

She shivered at the look on his face— that of a person who'd lost touch with reality.

Suddenly his knees buckled.

Alice screamed and scooted backward as fast as she could so he didn't land on her.

The man fell unconscious at her feet.

Drawing in a deep breath, she looked up and spotted Walt holding a cast iron skillet.

"Thank you, Walt. Thank you so much."

He grinned. "I owed him that. He tried to kill me and nearly succeeded. Twice. Remember?"

"Yes, I do." She looked around her and saw Melly kicking Lane.

"Don't you hurt my mama."

"Melly." She held out her arms. "Come here sweet, baby."

"I not a baby."

"You're right you're not. You are my

big girl. You and Walt saved Mama."

Her daughter needed her now.

Melly threw her arms around her mother's neck and burst into tears.

"He's a bad man."

Alice wrapped her arms tightly around her daughter and rocked as best she could.

"Yes, he is a bad man, but Jeremiah and Sam will take care of him."

The side door burst open and Jeremiah rushed into the room.

"Alice. Melly. Are you all right?" he called seeing them on the floor.

"Daddy," hollered Melly. "Me and Granpa Walt saved Mama."

Jeremiah stopped still.

"Did you just call me Daddy?"

"Yup." She put her arm around her mama's neck and looked down. "Is that okay?"

"I think it's wonderful."

He picked up his daughter and hugged her tight.

Walt was tying up Dick, so he couldn't get away when he woke up.

Alice couldn't have been happier.

"Uh, Jeremiah."

He looked up from nuzzling Melly.

"Yes, dear?"

"I'm having a contraction."

Jeremiah set Melly on the floor and went to kneel by Alice's side. "Do you think it's real labor or false brought on by the exertion?"

"The exertion. I'm sure if I rest for a bit, I'll be right as rain. Would you help me up, please?"

"Certainly."

He held his out his hands.

She grasped them and allowed him to pull her up off the floor.

"Where is Sam?"

"He wasn't there. I left a message for him with Jo. He'll be here as soon as he can."

Jeremiah put his arm around Alice's shoulders and steered her toward the stairs.

"I want you to get comfortable."

"I'm taking Melly with me upstairs. You and Walt stay here and wait for Sam." *I'm not about to let my baby out of my sight.*

"Melly should stay here with Walt. Sam will come as soon as he gets my message."

"Really, I'm fine. I…oh!"

Alice grabbed her stomach and bent over. The contraction was really hard. Not at all what she expected. It was too soon. The baby wasn't due for another two months.

"Alice?"

"I think the altercation has sped up the process. Walt you take Melly—"

"We're on our way to the other room. Come on, Melly girl," said Walt as he picked up the child and went out the door.

"I'm taking you upstairs."

Jeremiah lifted her into his arms and carried her to their bedroom where he sat her on the bed.

He unbuttoned her dress and slipped it off her shoulders.

She batted at his hands. "I can undress myself. I'm not an invalid."

"Of course, you're not. I'm just being helpful."

"Well stop."

"Yes, ma'am. I'll prepare the bed."

He stepped back and while she finished undoing her dress, he turned back the blankets.

Another contraction hit her just as she dropped her dress to the floor. Alice fell back onto the bed.

"Okay, maybe I do need some help. I'm sorry I was peevish before."

He smiled. "I'm not going anywhere. I don't care how contrary you get."

Jeremiah finished undressing her and then put a nightgown over her head.

The contraction ended and she was breathing easier. Leaning a hand on the mattress, she stood, then pulled the garment down over her body.

He stacked the pillows in the middle of the bed so she'd have them against her back.

Holding out his hand, he said, "Come lie down. You'll feel better."

She took his hand and sat on the side of the bed before scooting to the middle and lying down, a bit out of breath.

"There. Isn't that better?"

She nodded. "I'm not ready for her now. She can't come yet. She'd never survive."

He sat on the side of the bed and rubbed her feet, relaxing her even more.

"Everything will be fine once you relax. I'll get the pillows from the spare room and prop up your feet."

"Ah, that feels wonderful. You can stop in a week."

He chuckled. "I'll be right back."

She moaned and sank deeper into the pillows.

"Will you love our child?"

He frowned and stopped rubbing her feet. "Of course, I will. What kind of question is that?"

"Well, I know you love Melly, but you don't love me, I just wondered…" She looked away, her eyes swimming with tears.

"Alice. I was an ass. I was afraid to love you, afraid of being hurt. But I've watched you put your love out on a platter for me. I've watched you take chances and, even when I refused to return the emotion, you continued to love me."

She held her breath, hoping he'd go further and make the declaration she's been yearning to hear.

"Are you still afraid?"

"No. I've learned that I have no need to fear and I can admit that I've loved you for the longest time. I've watched you take in Walt and make him a part of our family. And how you treat every patient with tender care, as though they were your own sister, brother or child. How can I not love such a caring, giving woman?"

Her chest, no longer tight, she sighed. She took the necklace from around her neck and gave it to Jeremiah.

"I don't need this anymore. I love you, too, Jeremiah, with all my heart. I want to keep it for Melly, but I will never wear it again."

He took the chain and shoved it in his pocket. "I'll put it away for her."

"Oh, Jeremiah. You've made me so happy. I ah—"

She closed her eyes and held her belly, letting her breath out slowly.

"You better let me check you. I'm afraid he might be ready to join us."

"Not yet. Even the fight with Lane won't have started the baby coming now. I won't let it."

"Let me check to be sure."

He stood.

"Raise your knees and open your legs for me."

She obeyed.

"Well, you're not dilating, so that's a good thing. We've just got to keep you calm and relaxed."

He lay down beside her and gathered her against him.

"You amaze me. You're having contractions and still able to spar with me about the sex of our child."

"I can for now, but when the time comes, I'll probably be calling you every name in the book, but that will not be today."

"And when the time comes, I will accept those names with grace."

"Thank you, for loving me, for saving Melly and me."

"How could I not? Loving you is easy."

\*\*\*\*\*

An hour later, Alice was feeling better and the contractions had stopped. She put on her wrapper and went downstairs to be with her family.

There was a quick knock at the kitchen door and then Sam rushed in the house.

"I see you took care of him. Who took him down?" asked Sam.

"Walt and Melly," said Alice proudly

"Well now." Sam rocked back on his heels. "I know there's a story there and I intend to hear it just as soon as I get this man into my jail."

Dick Lane moaned.

Sam bent over him and untied his wrists from his ankles. "Good. He's coming around, but I need him to walk. I'm sure as heck not carrying him to jail."

Alice laughed. It felt good to laugh. Good to finally have this behind her and be free to come and go as she pleased. Good to never have to worry about him coming after her or her family again.

"I'll see you all later. If I were you, I'd close the office for a day or two and relax after this experience." Sam led his prisoner out of the house.

"That's not a bad idea," said Jeremiah.

She looked up at him.

He was staring down at her.

"I love you."

She said the words and meant them more than she ever had. She'd loved Adam, yes, but that was the love of children. Her love for Jeremiah was deeper than anything she'd felt for Adam. Stronger. Wilder.

Alice had never been happier than she was in Hope's Crossing, with her forever love.

# EPILOGUE

February 1874

"Ha! Oh! Jeremiah!" She squeezed his hand so tight she was afraid she broke it. "Ohhh."

As the contraction subsided, she tried to relax, breathing deeply. She continued to hold Jeremiah's hand, unwilling to let it go for even a minute.

"I'm a doctor. I'm supposed to be made of stronger stuff than I appear to be. These contractions are so hard. They weren't this strong with Melly, this early on."

"With this baby you're dilating quickly. He'll be here in a few hours."

Six hours later

Jeremiah placed a towel under her bottom to be ready for the baby.

"How are you doing, sweetheart? The baby is starting to crown. I want you to push now, love. Push hard."

She held on to the bars in the headboard for leverage and pushed as hard as she could.

"Okay. That's good. Rest a minute. Breathe deeply. Ready? Now push! Harder that's it. Push. Push. Push."

She sweated like a pig even her scalp was damp and her fingers ached from hanging on the bars on the iron headboard.

"Jeremiah, you bastard, you push and see how you like it."

"That's right sweetheart. I love you, too. Now, push. My son is almost here."

"My daughter," she ground out.

He laughed. "All right, your daughter is almost here. Push."

Her body ached. She felt like she was being torn asunder as the baby came out a little at a time.

"That's it, his head is out, a few more pushes and he'll be here. Come on, sweetheart, you can do it."

"I'm so tired, Jeremiah. So tired."

"I know you are but give me just one more big push. Come on, push."

The baby slipped out into Jeremiah's hands.

"That's my girl. We have a beautiful son."

"We do. A boy?"

His neck was bent, looking at their son. "Didn't I just tell you so?"

Tears rolled down her cheeks. "Give me my baby."

"Let me clean him up a little."

She watched her loving husband carry their son to the bureau and lay the baby on a towel. Then he poured water into the basin, took a washcloth, dipped it in the water and cleaned the baby's face and mouth.

A tiny cry issued from the babe. As his father continued to clean the birthing away, the baby whimpered.

"There," said Jeremiah to his son. "All better. Now you're ready to meet your mama."

"I can't wait."

She held up her arms, eager to hold her son.

He set the baby into her hands.

She brought him to her stomach and laid him there. Together they examined him. Counting his little fingers and toes. She ran her palm lightly over his blond hair. It was drying quickly and sticking straight up where his daddy had rubbed him with the towel.

"He's going to look like his mama."

"And his sister."

She reached up and palmed Jeremiah's jaw.

"I'm so glad you got your son. I had a feeling the baby would be a boy, but I couldn't let you think I agreed with you. What if he had been a girl? You would have been disappointed, and I didn't want that to happen."

"I know."

"You knew? How?"

"You were so persistent, and you always had a smile when you said it. You were just arguing with me to be arguing."

"Mostly. Now what are we going to name this little one?"

"I can't believe we haven't discussed our parents names before now. What was your father's name?"

"Earl. But I don't want to name this

baby Earl. Poor thing. What was your father's name?"

"Raymond. Same as my middle name."

"What do you think? Raymond Kilarney?"

He shook his head, a small frown crossed his face. "How about James? We can call him Jamie."

Alice looked down at her baby son. He had a little cleft in his chin that the girls would all find quite adorable when he was a man.

"James Kilarney. James Raymond Kilarney. I like it."

"Then so be it. I'll fill out the paperwork…later…much later."

He settled back against the headboard and watched as Alice put the baby to her breast and urged him to nurse.

"You should go get Melly and Walt. Let them know the baby is here and to come and meet him."

He kissed her lightly on the lips. "Be right back."

After he left, Alice gazed at her blue-eyed baby. She knew that most babies had blue eyes and they could change as he got older or they might stay blue. She hoped that the family trait of violet eyes was passed down to him. The girls would never let him be.

"You'll be a heart-breaker no matter what color your eyes are, my Jamie, love. Mama loves you. Mama loves Daddy, too."

She kissed the baby's stomach and then his lips and the top of his head before putting him to her shoulder.

"I'm very glad to hear that you love me, too. Because I love you so much, Alice Kilarney. I can't imagine my life without you."

Alice looked up, mouth agape.

He seemed to understand her confusion.

"I met them on the stairs."

Alice lifted her head in understanding.

"Melly," said her mother. "Come meet your baby brother."

The little girl walked over to the bed and Jeremiah lifted her so she could see Jamie.

She wrinkled her brow. "He's awful wittle."

Alice smiled and Jeremiah chuckled.

"Yes, he is tiny and he's depending on you to be his big sister and help him learn things as he gets older. Do you think you can do that?" asked Alice.

Melly pursed her lips and thought about it for a minute, then nodded. "Yup. I can do that and Granpa Walt can help me."

"That's true," said Walt. "I'll do whatever she wants to help the little tyke."

"Come closer so you can see him, Walt," said Alice.

Walt had been hanging back.

"He needs to meet his grandpa, too."

The little family surrounded the bed, looking at the newest addition. Alice was moved to tears. When she signed up to be a mail-order bride she never expected to find love. She'd only hoped to find a place where she could practice medicine and raise her daughter.

She had found so much more. Jeremiah had turned into her knight in shining armor, whether he wanted to or not. Walt was the most surprising addition to her family and one she was especially happy with because he'd saved not only her daughter's life but her own as well. And he loved Melly. That was all she could ask for.

Her life was more wonderful than she'd ever imagined.

She reached up and caressed Jeremiah's face, wrapped her hand around his neck and brought his head down to hers. Alice put all the love she had into the kiss and felt it returned.

Smiling she closed her eyes in contentment.

Jeremiah leaned down and kissed the top of her head.

"Have I told you lately how lucky I am to have my unexpected bride?"

"Unexpected?"

"I never expected a doctor or a woman that I could love with all my heart."

"I love you, too. Melly and I were the lucky ones. You could have sent us back, but you didn't. I love you, Jeremiah Kilarney, more than I ever thought possible."

She leaned her head back and his lips found hers. The kiss, gentle and fierce, held all the joy and promise for an incredible future in a place known as Hope's Crossing. Where hopes and dreams really do come true.

# ABOUT THE AUTHOR

Cynthia Woolf is the award winning and best-selling author of twenty-seven historical western romance books and two short stories with more books on the way.

Cynthia loves writing and reading romance. Her first western romance Tame A Wild Heart, was inspired by the story her mother told her of meeting Cynthia's father on a ranch in Creede, Colorado. Although Tame A Wild Heart takes place in Creede that is the only similarity between the stories. Her father was a cowboy not a bounty hunter and her mother was a nursemaid (called a nanny now) not the ranch owner. The ranch they met on is still there as part of the open space in Mineral County in southwestern Colorado.

Writing as CA Woolf she has six scifi, space opera romance titles. She calls them westerns in space.

Cynthia credits her wonderfully supportive husband Jim and her great critique partners for saving her sanity and allowing her to explore her creativity.

# TITLES AVAILABLE

THORPE'S MAIL-ORDER BRIDE, Montana Sky Series (Kindle Worlds)
KISSED BY A STRANGER, Montana Sky Series (Kindle Worlds)

GENEVIEVE: Bride of Nevada, American Mail-Order Brides Series

THE HUNTER BRIDE – Hope's Crossing, Book 1
THE REPLACEMENT BRIDE – Hope's Crossing, Book 2
THE STOLEN BRIDE – Hope's Crossing, Book 3
THE UNEXPECTED BRIDE – Hope's Crossing, Book 4

GIDEON – The Surprise Brides

MAIL ORDER OUTLAW – The Brides of Tombstone, Book 1
MAIL ORDER DOCTOR – The Brides of Tombstone, Book 2
MAIL ORDER BARON – The Brides of Tombstone, Book 3

NELLIE – The Brides of San Francisco 1
ANNIE – The Brides of San Francisco 2
CORA – The Brides of San Francisco 3
SOPHIA – The Brides of San Francisco 4
AMELIA – The Brides of San Francisco 5

JAKE (Book 1, Destiny in Deadwood series)
LIAM (Book 2, Destiny in Deadwood series)
ZACH (Book 3, Destiny in Deadwood series)

CAPITAL BRIDE (Book 1, Matchmaker & Co. series)
HEIRESS BRIDE (Book 2, Matchmaker & Co. series)
FIERY BRIDE (Book 3, Matchmaker & Co. series)

TAME A WILD HEART (Book 1, Tame series)
TAME A WILD WIND (Book 2, Tame series)
TAME A WILD BRIDE (Book 3, Tame series)
TAME A HONEYMOON HEART (novella, Tame series)

WEBSITE – http://cynthiawoolf.com/

NEWSLETTER - http://bit.ly/1qBWhFQ

DISCARD

76272721R00148

Made in the USA
Middletown, DE
11 June 2018